The Cello Player

MICHAEL KRÜGER

The Cello Player

Translated from the German
by Andrew Shields

HARCOURT, INC.

ORLANDO AUSTIN NEW YORK

SAN DIEGO TORONTO LONDON

www.HarcourtBooks.com

This is a translation of *Die Cellospielerin*

Library of Congress Cataloging-in-Publication Data
Krüger, Michael, 1943–
[Cellospielerin. English]
The cello player / Michael Krüger;
translated from the German by Andrew Shields.
p. cm.
ISBN 0-15-100591-5
I. Shields, Andrew. II. Title.
PT2671.R736C4513 2004
833'.914—dc21   2003013369

Text set in Dante
Designed by Scott Piehl

Printed in the United States of America

First U.S. edition
A C E G I K J H F D B

The Cello Player

I

There was no cemetery as far as the eye could see. The taxi driver, a heavy, sullen man with a bird face, made a vague gesture with his right hand in response to my question about where I should go, but without speaking; he was silent now, having spent the entire ride addressing with growing impatience a radio show and the tattered, rattling voice of the dispatcher. I should have asked the friendly taxi driver who had brought me from the Budapest airport to the hotel an hour earlier to wait after all. He had offered me everything—young women, nightclubs, gypsy music: You say, I get. But I'd wanted to rest for ten minutes before the funeral, so I sent him off. Where is the cemetery? I implored the bird man, from the backseat, while he calmly lit another cigarette on the stub of the old one, sending a shower of sparks onto his loosely knit sweater. He had stopped under a tree whose sooty leaves hung limply from its branches; behind the tree was a dilapidated square where an old car without wheels was sulking; in the distance were a few cowering

2 ~ MICHAEL KRÜGER

houses. No people and no graves in this wasteland. Fortunately, the hotel porter had written down the address of the cemetery for me, so now, with the driver gazing at me suspiciously, I looked for the slip of paper as I sat in the oppressive, cramped vehicle, which was full of smoke and incomprehensible sounds. I was beginning to sweat. I had assumed as a matter of course that taxi drivers in this part of the world cheated their fares—an assumption that the hotel porter had confirmed by pocketing a sizable tip— still, the thought that this deadly driver would abandon me in this no-man's-land simply for his own amusement was more than I could bear. And yet, I couldn't afford to annoy him, for there were hardly any other cars in the area, let alone taxis; but above all, there was no cemetery. I looked for the note; the man kept smoking and coughing, then he opened the car door and spat a heavy glob of phlegm on the dusty ground. The situation was so outrageous and humiliating that I was just about to shout the name of the hotel at the man and demand that I be taken back to my starting point when I finally found the note crumpled up in the breast pocket of my suit and triumphantly held it out to him. Here, the address of the cemetery, I urged the laconic fellow, who peered at the unprepossessing document out of the corner of his eye and nodded thoughtfully. He started the car and again began a steady muttering and carrying-on, as if he had put the ignition key into his speech center. The view outside the cab did not improve, particularly as a fine rain began to fall, covering the dreary neighborhood with a gray mist. Any hope I'd had of arriving at the cemetery a half-hour before the burial—not only to get a sense of where the grave was but also to explore possible escape routes—dissolved as I rode in my smoky cage. I wondered if we would ever arrive. Then the driver pulled into a gas station, shouting and snorting, and stopped beside a pump that did not look especially promising. He got out, fumbled at the back with the tailgate, and then disappeared for some time. I finally caught sight of him behind the car, tearing large chunks from an enormous sandwich he held in one hand and guzzling a cloudy liquid, probably cider, from a bottle he held in the other. As he stood there chewing and drinking in front of the radiator, I noticed that the left side of his face was disfigured by a red, frayed patch of eczema that spread over his eye and ran down his neck under the collar of his greasy sweater. As he made no effort at all to fill the tank, and no attendant put in an appearance, I energetically pushed my coat, suit, and shirt-sleeves from my wrist and tapped several times on my watch with my right index finger, assuming this gesture must be recognizable anywhere in the world. Not a twitch of comprehension in his face. But once the last of the sandwich had vanished into his maw and the bottle had been stowed in the trunk he decided it was time to fill up his tank. When at last the counter on the pump had come to a halt while there was still a chance of reaching our destination, for which we had set out more than an hour ago, the man tore open the door on my side and barked furiously at me. That could only be about money, I thought. So I pulled out the bundle of bills that a tired woman in the hotel had given me in exchange for my hundred marks, and put a medium-sized bill into the outstretched palm. But the hand did not close on the bill. Nor did it close after I had put two more on top of the first. By then, a group of ragged people had stepped closer, forming a half-circle around the driver and watching the silent transaction. Among them was a woman with a pom-pom hat who shamelessly thrust her shaggy head into the car and reached out her hand to snatch one of the bills. I had no idea how much money I had handed over or how much I was still holding, nor did the hostile maneuvers I found myself subjected to give me time to figure it out. I had to act. The only way out of this situation was to attack. I pulled myself out of the backseat with the bundle of remaining money firmly in hand, stood up, legs apart, in front of the group of people gathered around the taxi driver, paused for a moment, then screamed as loud as I could: If I am not taken to the cemetery at once, I'll have the police throw all of you in jail! And as I kept on screaming, rousing myself with the worst profanities and proud of the courage I never knew I had, I butted my fist into the chests of the flabbergasted men and, with a swipe, knocked the shameless pom-pom hat from the woman's head. Even the driver seemed impressed. Don't stop now; don't drop the reins. In my mounting rage, I was about to go for the throat of the crimson bird-head when a little oil-smeared man stepped between us and, in excellent German, asked about the cause of this violent confrontation. I want to go to the cemetery, I yelled; where the hell is the goddamn cemetery this idiot refuses to take me to, even though he has already taken wads of money from me! It's a scandal for a visitor to be treated like this; the simplest rules of hospitality have been violated; all of Hungary is being infiltrated by scoundrels who are entirely ignorant of the laws of civilization. . . .

Cemetery? Cemetery? asked the oily man. You want to go to the cemetery? And, with a friendly smile, he folded me up again and pushed me into the backseat, while the taxi driver with the eczema got behind the wheel again, started the car, and, to the applause of the fascinated spectators, headed back into the road—which, after a few minutes, actually took us to the cemetery. You wait here, I ordered the bird man. Wait, you understand? I pointed at my watch, raised two fingers, and again said, Wait, here. There was no more talk of money. And when, after buying a wreath from a sweet, toothless little woman, I turned to check on my taxi, I just caught a glimpse of it chugging and banging around the corner. Thank God, I thought, things have turned out all right, and, as I assumed that I had saved a lot of money by losing the greedy taxi driver, I pressed another bill into the rough hand of the graveyard woman.

The rain grew heavier. Outside the crumbling consecration hall, the puddles were too large to jump and one had to wade through them. A man in a uniform stood smiling outside the door, like an escort for the dead, observing the visitors' vain efforts to keep their feet dry. What care we take at the end!

In the middle of the puddle, discouraged, I turned around, stood on my heel, awkwardly took a larger leap, and ran across dry ground into the cemetery, my feet wet in my sopping shoes. Only after I had sprinted for a while, as if a destination were drawing me through the apparently infinite expanse of the cemetery, did I finally regain my composure. The silent order of the stones, most of them old and crooked comrades arching over Austrian bones, slowed my steps to a calmer gait, and my thoughts to a less erratic excitement. After ten minutes of walking, my hands clasped behind my back, I was already on such familiar terms with death that I was able to sit down on a tiny bench beside a disheveled grave to smoke a cigarette. It had stopped raining. The clouds were twisted into bizarre shapes by a rising wind; right above me they looked like a bear standing upright with raised paws. At the edge of the stone, which guarded the remains of one Martha Lunkewicz, mushrooms were growing, pale honey mushrooms like those in cemeteries in Berlin, but firmer, and still, barely, edible. Martha had given up the ghost in 1956—or had no choice: with that year in mind, which of the two was unclear. She had been in the world for nineteen years. Why wasn't her birthplace carved on the stone?

Though I was aware that I didn't belong here, I felt comfortable on my low, ramshackle bench, whose legs had burrowed deep into the ground while my own feet, wet, rested on the speckled ivy. I placed the pack of cigarettes on the gravestone, which made the sullen stone look as if it were wearing a red cap; I carefully pushed my smoked-out butts into the mulch. Maybe Martha and Maria were once friends. Martha's father was perhaps Polish, a Party member; her mother might have been from Budapest. Maybe they were neighbors and played music together. Martha, the older of the two, in a faded velvet dress inherited from her grandmother, a brooch pinned to her breast, sat at the piano; Maria, in worn white socks, played the violin. Every Tuesday and Friday from two to four; the neighbors did not allow more. Martha very focused in spite of the out-of-tune piano, and sometimes indignant when her younger companion did not keep time well. Bartók. After they finished playing, they stood for a while together at the window and silently looked out at the street. What do you see? I see nothing, would be the answer, absolutely nothing. And when the conservatory is behind us, what do you think our lives will be like? We will live in Paris, Martha said, and there will be no car with two men sitting in it, rolling down the window every eight minutes and throwing cigarette butts into the street. Why do policemen smoke all the time?

Once, in a hotel in Warsaw, I caught Maria staring out the window as if she had turned to stone, her raised right arm bent across the pane at an angle, her left hand supporting her on the windowsill. When I came in, I knew she was crying, because the pane was fogging under the red mane of her hair, creating a milky circle whose circumference grew with every breath, then shrank again. When I stepped up behind her and asked what was going on, she pointed to a car across the street. There were three men sitting in it smoking, and at that very moment they rolled down the windows and flicked out the butts, which went out in the slush with a tiny spray of sparks. My childhood—I could get nothing more out of her.

Judit, too, would stand at the window and look out, even when she was talking to me. A magnetic attraction, a genetic compulsion that pulled her to the window long after the enemy had stopped sitting in the car outside and was standing at her back, in the room, one breath away. If

Judit had been observed from the street at moments of terrible torment, as she stood at the window with her arms raised and her features distorted, she would have been taken for an actress rehearsing Medea, or simply for a madwoman. And when she pressed her forehead or the palms of her hands against the pane, to distract herself for a few seconds, the image of imprisonment was complete. Once, while arguing with me, she slammed the case of a CD of Beethoven's complete piano concertos so violently against the frame, in time with her rage, that the disk shattered, right at the rondo of the second concerto.

Perhaps, I thought, as I sat by the grave of this Martha whom I didn't know, perhaps Judit had instinctively sensed that because of her attachment to Maria, which was nothing but a dependence that inspired imitation bordering on the ridiculous, she was incapable of becoming an independent artist. She would always remain the perfect imitation, the double of a brilliant mother. Aren't you Maria's daughter? Perhaps the hypochondriac presumption of her desire to drag me, of all people, into her circle was nothing but an attempt to step out of Maria's shadow without having to separate from her, because Judit was entirely convinced that I would never summon up the courage to creep away from Maria's halo, whether I was living with other women or alone. I was infected. Incurably infected, for life. Perhaps Judit had hoped to hide from Maria with me. On the other hand, she was too intelligent for such games.

Poor Martha Lunkewicz. She had to listen to all these ruminations blubbered out at her grave by a shell of a man. And yet that wasn't enough. One question hung over everything: why had Judit chosen me? God knows there were other figures in her mother's life whom she could have appropriated for her purposes. Directors, pianists, composers, critics: all those invalids of an ailing culture who had a good cry with Maria and let her console them, all those immature, famous men who now masterfully delight concert audiences were at her disposal and would undoubtedly have been thrilled to be harnessed to Judit's moods. What made her turn to a man overcome by the demon of failure, to someone down for the count, who had finally made peace with himself because he no longer wanted anything? Perhaps she had sought somebody on whom she could impose her notion of victory. She needed a loser as a guinea pig, someone she could easily defeat. She always had to win. If we went to a concert and an acquaintance did not greet her, she would remain standing until she was recognized, after I was already sitting and reading the program. At the intermission, while I was still clapping she'd be pushing her way out of the hall, to be first into the foyer and be seen by everyone right away. And when she finally found someone who, dazed and at a loss, was still listening in his mind to what he had just heard, she would launch into a lecture about the musicians and the composition until nothing but words of agreement could be heard. A Stockhausen piece I heard with her comes to mind, a badly devised composition that even the most valiant of musicians had found no way to hold together. During the intermission, Judit gathered a circle of young people around us and explained to them, in a strident voice but with fluttering gestures, why we had just heard a masterpiece, and she actually did manage, in all of fifteen minutes, to heat up the atmosphere so much that the astonished musicians received frenetic, utterly exaggerated applause at the end of the program.

The Marlboro pack was empty. I dropped the last lighted match on the grave of Martha Lunkewicz, where it went out with a hiss. Peace to your bones. A timid sun, which provided a bit of warmth, fought its way through the clouds. When I stood up, I heard my joints crack. An old man at a stranger's grave in a cemetery in Budapest. I buttoned my coat with excessive care and bowed slightly to the grave, whose resident had been forced to overhear a pointless self-interrogation. To unlock the secret, I had to recall the whole story again, day by day. There had to be a key.

I turned around and saw a funeral procession approaching through the sparse trees and bushes. That had to be them. A swarm of black bees behind a flower-covered coffin in a black wooden cart, the wheels grinding on the worn-down gravel. I quickly turned up my coat collar, put the empty cigarette pack in my pocket, and ran toward the exit. I did not belong here; that was for sure.

At the entrance to the cemetery, cigarette burning in the corner of his mouth, stood the taxi driver, his blood-red rash shining in the pallid sun.

2

There is an hour in the day when all the important decisions in my life are made (insofar as they are subject to conscious planning and not merely the result of random events): namely, between six and seven in the morning. With frightening regularity, I wake up at six o'clock; sometimes I can even see the second hand on my watch hurrying toward the twelve and producing the straight line I consider the only truly straight line in my life.

What comes after seven o'clock is purely managerial in nature: mere melancholy consummation. If I have a complicated sequence of notes in my head in the morning, it disintegrates over the course of the day and is wiped out by evening. If, in the morning, I resolve to break all my ridiculous commitments and leave a state of ambiguity for one of clarity, the day provides a thousand reasons to make the transition gentle, and before supper I have already resigned myself to everything remaining as it was, for the time being at least. Only in this one hour do I feel free; the rest of the day is agony, the petrified imprint of that productive restlessness that comes over me right after I wake up. That explains why I have never really been interested in my dreams, not even in the days when the whole world bent over backward to interpret the shadow theater of the soul for all sorts of reasons. "Psychoanalysis and Music"— I attended that lecture often, along with all the pretty students. Why had the petite blonde chosen the harp she pressed so trustingly between her thighs? Why did the stocky, pimply fellow from Münster blow his sparse breath into a trombone? And why did Beethoven decide one day that he did not want to hear his own sounds anymore? Even the issue of whether Schubert had homosexual tendencies troubled my generation. "The Effect of Drive Renunciation on Artistic Achievement" was the seminar everybody wanted to attend. Through the act of "overhearing," the seminar concluded, the composer forces the listeners to acknowledge the guilt that compelled him to compose. So we were accomplices. And when particular pieces by Schubert drove us to tears, we were really experiencing the composer's remorse. Just imagine what sins lay on Stockhausen's shoulders! A parallel nightmare was the elaborate lecture on "Marxism and Music," another course everybody felt obliged to attend. The climax of those years came when a fusion of the two was offered: "The Influence of Psychoanalysis and Marxism on Musical Development: The Instinctual Life of Sounds as the Expression of the Bad Conscience of Industrial Late Capitalism, as seen in Stravinsky and Schönberg." All obsessive-compulsives, that was clear. How had all these beautiful theories withered away?

If one were to offer such courses today, thirty years later, one would probably be declared insane. I don't know a single musician who has read more than a line of Freud or Marx. Back then, one had to; there was no excuse not to. And in the breaks between those now forgotten spectacles in the typical humanities education, everyone sat together relating dreams from the night before. I was the only one who had nothing to contribute. Moreover I was silent when ridiculed for my refusal: I had a screw loose when it came to sex, I was repressing, they said, or I was just a spoilsport.

They all nod their heads knowingly when I talk about my inner clock. That's common knowledge! Biologist friends have sent me studies of the inner clock in birds and insects. But they can't possibly know how agonizing such compulsive waking is, the torture of having to look the world in the eye at a certain time of day, quite apart from the effect on planning one's day and one's life that comes with such a biological constant. For of course, I don't go to bed at eleven in the evening because I look forward to getting up early, nor do I leave the bottle of red wine half empty in order to have a clear head in the morning, and it is utterly impossible for me to tailor my creative work to the barbaric boundary my genes have planted in my body. After a great deal of training, however, I learned, while still a schoolboy, to close my eyes right after opening them and to keep them closed for an hour, and during this hour I take the time every day, even now, to consider my affairs and—as far as I can—to make decisions. Even my work as a composer takes place at that hour; what follows is nothing but figuring out the details, putting on the finishing touches. That might be connected to the fantastic sense that I am only myself during that hour. In all the other hours I spend awake, I have to compete, which leads me to be tempted, several times a day, to throw in the towel. Every artist looks for something that distinguishes him from the others. And as it never takes long for him to realize that he is not that different from anyone else, he keeps inventing new tricks and feints to make something special of his normality. Some live their whole lives that way. They invent concertos for six pianos and one oboe, then complain if these works are promptly forgotten. As for me, I haven't invented anything. But I have something that, clearly, no one can take from me: the hour between six and seven. The rest of the day dissolves and disintegrates, and all my attempts at discipline, from regular mealtimes and working hours to the walks I've been told to take, have fallen through after a few weeks. Sometimes I wonder what would happen if this hour were stolen from me by an illness. I would simply shut down.

I owe the two decisions I made to get married, as well as the divorces that ended those generally depressing unions, to this hour, along with all measures concerning my work. Incidentally, both my wives worked, in a touchingly caring way, on structuring my day, my life; both presented me with good, convincing strategies, from a planned diet to fixed holidays, from regular visits to the doctor to physical fitness, but all their well-intended methods, whether applied openly or not so openly, were of no use at all so long as the heart of my day remained undiscovered, the secret organizer that alone made decisions about what

I had to do or not do possible. If it was decided at 6:30 A.M. that I would work on the piano pieces after all, that could well mean I would work on them for up to twelve hours without stopping, without a care for anything else; if there was no guideline about work, I would often lounge around all day long, rummaging through old projects or aimlessly reading the books that were multiplying as if by magic and, since my second wife had moved out, making themselves at home where they had not been tolerated before, in the kitchen and in the bathroom. Like an incurable disease, the books took over the apartment, and the threat now talked about everywhere—that the age of the book was coming to an end—seemed only to heighten their powers of resistance. How often I had resolved to give them some semblance of order. Music books in the music room, German literature in the bedroom, the Latin classics in the bay window, history in the hallway, poetry in the walk-in pantry, which, following the divorce, was left empty again. My unfortunate penchant for neatness had compelled me to start cartons for undecided cases, and now they, too, were spread out on the floor, only to be put into whatever space happened to be available. Lucretius could be found beside Mandelstam's essays in the Russian section, and I had a suspicion they enjoyed being neighbors. Actually, there was nothing more beautiful than stumbling around among the books, reading the day away, and so long as the demands of German television for terrible theme songs made such a life possible, I didn't argue. I enjoyed my laziness without thinking about success. Certainly I was hurt that my "Passages through Time for

Piano and Oboe" did not get the recognition it deserved, with its complex and beautiful development. And of course, the fact that my two operas had been performed only once in Germany (and only occasionally abroad) upset me too. On the other hand, I was happy that my increasingly successful television compositions made it possible to do without a professorship and its regimen of responsibilities, something many of my colleagues worked hard to achieve. I was proud of being an independent artist, and my retirement plan was more than guaranteed by the clever, sympathetic manner of Detective Michalke, who solved a case once a month to the sound of my music. Along with my apartment, I owned two other condominiums and a summer house in France. My two wives had received fair settlements and I had no children. I had found a publisher for my serious music, who took care of it in his way; the most important song cycles, the quartets, and the piano pieces were available on records and CDs, and the Nuremberg Theater had given me a commission to compose my third opera, which was supposed to keep me busy for the next two years. I had loosely agreed to create the libretto with a writer from the neighborhood, but we were still looking for a subject. He came over in the afternoon sometimes for coffee, carrying piles of books, and by the time he left in the evening to see one of his many girlfriends, we could have taken over the repertory of all the opera houses in the world with our fantasies, but we still had not made a decision. He wanted to adapt a classic story, so he could pocket undivided royalties, but the plots he dredged up did not strike a chord with me. I didn't want to give voice to a Medea, I wanted to put one of the great tragic figures of modern poetry onstage (Tsvetayeva, Mandelstam, Pessoa), to create a final, powerful example before poetry took its leave, definitively disappearing into the archives of meaninglessness. But my writer wouldn't go along with that. First of all, it was not yet clear that poetry really would vanish; second, the problem was theoretical, and could not be staged; third, nobody in Nuremberg, let alone in New York or São Paulo, was interested in Pessoa's masks or Mandelstam's fate. Mandelstam's death—a theoretical problem? That was how we spent our afternoons, without ever writing a line, let alone a note, and that was fine. For it was, of course, clear from the beginning that it would be a Mandelstam opera. I had decided this one morning after I woke up. The rest was banter, killing time so as not to have to begin.

Every Mandelstam edition in every possible language lay ready in my study, which was accessible only to me and the cleaning lady. Photographs of the poet were arranged on all the bookshelves; next to them, marked with little flags, was the Soviet memoir literature, piled-up biographies of Stalin, and histories of the Revolution, along with a plethora of books on the aesthetics and history of Russian literature and collections of photographs, journals, and clippings from newspapers. The program for my opera was ready, it was just that the opera itself was taking its time. The song of the sirens was mute; I had tied myself to the mast in vain. I couldn't exactly appear as Odysseus and be celebrated by the very people who had their ears plugged with wax.

Why didn't I begin? Not because Günter, the librettist, wasn't ready to accept my ideas. Another problem was distracting me, a problem that had to be resolved in one of my morning hours. Shortly before Christmas—that is, about six months ago now—I received a letter from a Hungarian friend in Budapest, asking me to put in a good word for her daughter at the conservatory here. After finishing high school, Judit had been accepted for the cello course at the Budapest Conservatory, but for some reason that could not be gathered from the letter, she planned to leave the country and get her "finishing touches" in Germany. You must do this in the memory of our old love, Maria had written, and although I found the pathos of the letter embarrassing, and the appeal to our old love a clear attempt to manipulate me, I leaped into action right away, calling acquaintances at the school, requesting forms, and guaranteeing that I would support Judit if she did not receive a fellowship. On the day before Christmas Eve, in the most terrible mood, as I am every year at that time, I had finally pulled myself together enough to draft a response that was intended to describe Judit's prospects as formally as possible. Then, at four o'clock in the afternoon, a carbon copy of Maria as I had known her twenty years before appeared at the door. Servus, the copy said, and, given the resemblance, all else was irrelevant. Stunned, I was looking into a mirror in which hundreds more mirrors were reflected, and in every mirror I saw myself and Maria—in the concert hall and in bed; in the museum and in a Polish forest covered in deep snow as a storm performed a devilish symphony; on the shore of the sluggish Danube and in the deserted streets of Leipzig—and every image sparked repressed feelings, fleeting stimuli that threw me, at the endpoint of this labyrinthine gallery, into a state of total confusion. Come in, I finally said. Pick out a room and get some rest; we'll meet in the kitchen in an hour. As for me, I had to prepare myself for this comedy.

Now more than six months have passed, and Judit is still living in my apartment. Her demands are growing, and I urgently need to do something to get her out of my life.

3

It might be a relief to buy newspapers, I thought, if you don't know what else to do. As I went down the stairs in the darkness, I felt like someone on a voyage of discovery, creeping past the doors to the apartments I owned and finally stepping into the open, which to me seemed like an open field, an oasis of distraction. I had been sitting around in the cramped attic too long, in the milky smoke of countless cigarettes, a prisoner of my own stubbornness, whispering Mandelstam's lines to myself like magic spells:

Out of this space I walk, now,
Into the graves—a park run wild—
And rend what is constant, or seems so,
In causality, strengthened but ill.
I read the textbooks of the infinite,
Completely unaccompanied—
You blueless, wild book of medicine,
Of powerful roots still in seed.

But no redemption came, no mercy, no pity. Not even inspiration. Mandelstam's fate got in the way, his sad countenance in the last photographs. The poem was alone, with me outside it, and between us a narrow stretch of mud and knowledge that only vehemence and violence could bridge. I didn't become part of the lines, no matter how often I repeated them, and because I remained outside them, the music remained mute. As in a duel where no sign is given, words and music stood opposite each other, waiting, until they finally lost interest in each other. On the street, though, sequences of notes came to me as I walked, and I felt like going right back up the stairs to write an octave interval for flute and piano. But I didn't. One had to give a poet like Mandelstam time; under no circumstances should I overpower him.

Newspapers were going to save me—newspapers of all things.

I had clearly bought too many, for a hoarse voice from the *camera obscura* cut through the colorful images to demand over twenty marks. The kiosk owner was a dwarf. Her name was Frau Stier, the bull. I was surprised by how quickly she came up with the price, in spite of the fact that I had bought unusual publications—*El País, Le Monde,* and *The Guardian*—as well as the German weekend editions. I was curious as to whether the little festival in the Escorial would be mentioned. I wanted to see my name. Have you been mentioned again? asked the dwarf. Her twisted, scabbed hands rolled up the newspapers and bound them with a rubber band, snapping it with a little chirp. Her hands looked as if she had ragged gloves on. Without a word, I put the money on the glass tray, took the roll, and left without the ten that was shoved out of the peephole by a red claw. Was the dwarf married? I had never seen anyone else in the kiosk, just tiny Frau Stier with her thick mustache, sitting on a high swivel chair, which was visible only in the summer, when she left the back door open because of the heat. The first time I saw her I thought it was a child sitting there, whose short, heavy legs ended in sneakers. I had even thought of putting the kiosk onstage, on Red Square. Mandelstam would be sitting on an adjacent bench, reading about the absurdity of the world:

How weird everything is in the capital of smut:
The soil here is a hard, dry bread
And the impetuous, greedily grabbing market,
The robber Kremlin stands and threatens.

I sat down on a bench in the middle of the square. A tired fountain chattered softly to itself. With every gust of wind, a fine spray wafted across the square and made the people waiting for the bus raise their eyes. Every five minutes, a long wandering line of people came rolling out of the metro. When they reached the exit, the motionless masses broke into a run, as if they were on fire, casting reproachful looks at the people dozing on the benches. *Arise,* they seemed to say, *do not surrender your lazy souls to idleness—* but the people hunched on the benches didn't move.

I was at it for quite a while, separating the wheat from the chaff, observed by the watery eyes of a ragged little man. You read fast, he remarked of my increasingly hectic cleanup work, which prompted me to offer him a tall stack of paper. Thanks, he said, but I already have a great location. Then he pulled a little bottle of brandy from the inside pocket of his jacket and took a swig. Before he put it back, he held it up in front of himself to plan the afternoon better. Well then, was all he said.

I worked through the smaller pile, the heart of what had been printed, and whenever I came across a line that rubbed me the wrong way, I uttered this resigned *Well then*. Eventually I noticed that I was repeating myself. The chill of the falling evening seeped from the bench's iron bars into my body, but I couldn't stop. A few people were still standing on the pavement, but the traffic had slowed down and the little man had long since taken his leave. *Well then,* I finally said, as I reached the last page. I hadn't found my name.

What would actually happen if my generation were to stop composing? The world would certainly be the poorer for it. A lament would strike up, a demanding cry: Don't give up, keep going, we need new music like the air we breathe. Even if you think that every last conceivable variation has been run through, at least virtually, there is still a lot to do! There is a progress of sorts, even in music, that emerges from the material as an imperative. After constructive composing, there is deconstructive composing, so you can still be productive by following the path back to the beginning. In order to make that possible, the state, that most committed of all art machines, would introduce new composition classes; television would broadcast new operas twice a week; Bundestag deputies would listen to concertos for baritone, trumpet, and trombone before the sessions began; and popular street concerts for new music would be organized every weekend. Nothing is more popular than new music, after all, as a glance at concert programs reveals. There is hardly any more Beethoven or Mozart or Schubert; instead, we have new music everywhere. In the metro, kids read scores of Henze operas, and old people happily hum to themselves Schnebel's *Opus ultimum*. New music has truly become an event, an ongoing event for a society enthusiastic about music, which puts its own immobility back into motion with our sounds. We do what literature, art, and theater cannot do. If someone in Munich asks where Hercules Hall is, we need only point at the line of people winding through the city to grab a ticket for Wolfgang Rihm's new symphony. New music has become a pathological passion, and there are virtuosos of perception everywhere, discovering more music where none, seemingly, can be heard: shoes on the pavement, the sound of the last streetcars, the isolated ozone cough of a girl outside the Käfer department store—everything is music, sound, event. No, we must not give up; we must keep going; we are needed.

I shut my notebook so hard the music leapt out, startled. The world came from a hiccup and will end with a hiccup. Just as God tired of playing with dead matter, with glowing balls that buzzed around his head in more or less exact orbits, without visible deviation and without contingency, so will he tire of watching the ever-changing masquerades of people. And anyway, God doesn't understand new music. He stopped listening with Bach. When he hears our music, he plugs his ears with thick clouds. Cage's music seems like boundless narcissism to him, egocentric noise. But it is

God himself we have to thank for this predicament. After all, he was the one who wanted something always to be changing. He exhorted us not to close our minds to new listening habits, didn't he? It was he who told us there has to be something new, even after Bach, after Mozart, Schumann, and Schönberg, after Stockhausen and Boulez. So we got the violin out once more, and we plucked and bowed and beat and chopped again—and look, there actually was yet another small sequence of notes in the mess of noises, a tiny sequence, a whimpering arpeggio, that had never been heard before. Please, we said, here is something new, but he was not interested; he was still thinking about his well-tempered clavier. While he simplifies and impoverishes his stocks, he makes us chase the new, even though he knows exactly how it will end. There will be a final crash that all instruments will be part of, an enormous, exaggerated clamor of every imaginable sound. And then it will be quiet for a while. End of the concert, no more applause.

Perhaps it really was time to pack it in, time to close my bag and not wait anymore. No longer to hope that, among the rapidly changing fashions, one's own lifestyle would be in, just once. I could withdraw to France, and no one would notice my absence.

When we grew up in the sixties, we needed a new language to describe society and art. This was necessary because something new had emerged that could not be depicted in the old language. We did not have to distance ourselves from the old language and its speakers; we did not have to overthrow or destroy anyone. There was something before us that we alone perceived and tried to define. Only later did Marxism arrive, and it, too, was already an old song that could no longer express the new things beginning to assert themselves. The Marxism of the sixties was the nineteenth century's last attempt to get the second half of the twentieth century under control. I remembered the comical attempts to use Marxist terms to explain the naked cello player who sat on the stage under a transparent cellophane cover and made sounds. Marx would have been struck dumb and blind with horror, but we uttered the old junk fearlessly. Today, the new does not call for a new language. That must be why so much rhetorical effort is being put into slaughtering the present. With audible malice, with wit and cunning, the slaughter continues. Because nothing more lies ahead, everything that lies behind must be stomped. Hence the cynicism, the stupid jokes and puns, the trumped-up metaphors and images for something already gone, passé, dead.

A child walked past and cast a concerned look at the man who looked as if he had been snowed in by the wind-blown arts sections of various newspapers. Go away, I whispered through clenched teeth, get lost. The child kicked a ball against the outside wall of the fountain, over and over: Bounce right, you stupid ball, he said reproachfully, and the stupid ball appeared to be trying hard to obey. Suddenly it rolled to a stop at my feet, and I leaped up and kicked it with fury into the garden of the Residenz theater. The boy strolled over and looked at me with big eyes. Come on, I said cheerfully, let's go get the ball. I left the newspapers to the wind.

4

Judit had been sent to me, that much was clear. But what exactly was her mission? After just a few days, it was clear that she hadn't been sent to improve her cello playing. There probably wasn't anything she could learn here that she couldn't teach herself simply by practicing. Directly, with not a trace of tact or restraint, her presence in my apartment seemed focused on reproducing a previous situation. At first, to my amazement and then to my horror, she played the role of her mother. Her peculiar mix of vanity and arrogance, her capacity for rancor and malice, were derived from her mother. She also imitated Maria's tendency to esoteric practices. Even the finer registers of affection, from nuances to erratic tenderness, were copied. Judit was an artist of imitation, creating an illusion of the time when Maria and I had known each other. But why? For the falseness that Maria had mastered as no one else ever had was transparent in her imitation. And the more precisely and devotedly Judit played the part of her mother, the more obvious the lie became. Judit was playing an artist playing at truth because the truth was so banal and humiliating nobody wanted to waste any time on it. And, as before, I was expected to applaud. As a grown man, I was supposed to applaud my own youth, as played by Judit in the role of Maria.

Was that her mission?

5

For many years, I had been going to Madrid for two weeks in July to teach summer school. Accommodations were provided in a splendid, gloomy edifice in the old town, and the work involved only two hours of lessons every day, for no more than six students. Along with a princely sum, remuneration included a free pass to all museums and cultural institutions. But the main reason I so eagerly anticipated returning to Madrid every year was the prospect of spending fourteen days drifting incognito through the dives where gypsies played. Nowhere else in the world have I ever been able to forget myself so entirely. When the lights in a dim club were extinguished, and the gypsy band performed by the light of a few candles, I physically sensed life's small sorrows leaving my body, the wilting person I was at home becoming a fully concentrated listener, transformed by every nuance of the music. My general, never fully identifiable rage, which often mutated into a pitiful indifference, seemed to vanish in those cramped catacombs smelling of spilled wine. And the excess of boredom and melancholy that sometimes overcame me while working on my scores, the self-consciousness that prevented me from ever being able to write another spontaneous note, without cynicism, without corrosive skepticism, gave way to rapt attention when those mystics of passion filled the room with the sounds of their guitars, castanets, and voices. While I never allowed performances of modern music to touch me, in Madrid's gypsy bars I became entangled as deeply as possible. The wine did the rest. I usually began my nightly expeditions with the director of the music school, a woman whose name was, quite rightly in a way, Mercedes, but she only held out until dawn every third day. We would walk back together to the hotel, where, every time, startled by my own audacity, I would ask her to come to my room. There she would sing me to sleep with the saddest ballads. I am not sure whether she ever spent the night with me, and not even a glance into her eyes on seeing her the following afternoon could enlighten me on that score. If she responded to me, I was ashamed; if she said nothing, my shame still made me suffer. But no sooner would my lesson be over than I would be phoning to ask her to accompany me on my next tour. For three days in a row she would turn me down; then her resistance would yield. A bit dreamily, a tad coquettishly, she would sit with me again in the smoke-filled bars, listening to my rapture, drinking, smoking, and occasionally going outside with her phone to straighten out her family in Barcelona, before drinking again and then guiding me through the morning to our hostel, singing all the while. Maybe it was an emotional affinity that brought us together every year, but it was a safe relationship, with no false expectations. Since an ability to confide in other people is not one of my virtues, I never mentioned those nightly flamenco escapades to a soul, and as Mercedes was clearly not afraid of inappropriately surrendering her heart, we carried on with our peculiar game for years without ever being detected. The heart of our secret was the miraculous wealth of surprises the gypsy music granted us. A more innocent love affair could not be conceived. The superficiality that makes secrecy so tedious was unknown to us. If someone who didn't know better had seen us for only an instant they would have taken us for two strangers who happened to be sharing a table, chance acquaintances who would pay separately and disappear separately.

But now everything was different. My anticipation of the summer was marred by nervous restlessness, because my opera did not want to be written. My librettist, Günter, and I had both failed, there was no getting around it. And besides, Judit insisted on coming along. All my attempts to talk her out of the exhausting trip came to nothing. I have to work all day and talk to colleagues in the evening, I lied, but she triumphantly held up my schedule, which, negligently enough, I had hung up in the kitchen. And when, after long discussions, accompanied by fits of tears on her part, I presented my final argument—that I had to be alone again and that nowhere in the world could I be so completely alone as in Madrid—she accused me of simply wanting to get away from her, so that upon arrival in Madrid I could put an end to my solitude with another woman. I was on the verge of asking Mercedes to reserve me a second room for a companion, just to get Judit to leave me in peace, when one night she surprised me. After seeing a French film and then going to a bar with Günter, she announced that she had reconsidered: I could go alone. I sat at the kitchen table, clutching my wineglass; she stood in the doorway, her arms crossed and one leg bent, which she had probably just seen someone do in the movie. But I reserved a double, I said wearily. Then you'll have enough room to end your solitude, she responded maliciously. The rain dripped from her coat, forming a wet wreath on the kitchen floor. Do you want to know what film we saw? she asked. Although I muttered a loud and clear *no*, she related the story, down to the last detail, of a drama of jealousy that could only have been made in France—Catholic, insincere, and realistic—which naturally ended with the double murder of the adulterer and his mistress, sacrificed on the altar of their love, a bed in a shabby hotel to be precise, tangled up in each other. And the wife? I asked. What will the adulterer's wife do now, all alone in the world? She gets over it easily, Judit said, because now she can peacefully devote herself to her husband's best friend. He didn't happen to be Hungarian? I asked softly. And I don't suppose he was named Janos, like all the Hungarians who appear in French films?

One reason for Judit's sudden change of heart was that the preparations had to be made for her birthday celebration. Whenever she talked about the event, her face would light up unnaturally, only to make way for a worried expression that was just as unnatural. What that meant was unclear to me, and my questions brought no enlightenment—only a welter of hints. And she always closed her labyrinthine explanations with the childish assurance that her birthday party would be the most beautiful celebration we would ever have. She turned a deaf ear to my suggestion that we rent a nearby Italian restaurant, in order to spare the apartment, and also ignored my tentative attempt to talk her out of the party and into a trip to Paris. After my birthday, when my family has left, it would be lovely to go to Paris, with Janos, she said, and it sounded as if she assumed that her family would stay in my apartment for some time.

And your mother? I asked. Will Maria also grace us with her presence?

That depends on you, said Judit, who then bent over the invitation list and provided no further information.

So I went to Spain alone after all. To be safe, I left Judit my telephone number, and every morning, when I returned to my room, quite drunk and at odds with myself and the world, I would find a message that I should call Judit, who had tried to reach me every half-hour between midnight and two. I then sat for an eternity on the edge of the bed, but could not seem to manage to pick up the receiver and dial my own number. Tomorrow, I would mutter to myself, tomorrow I'll definitely call.

But I didn't. Until, just before returning home, Mercedes, who'd had too much work to guide me through the night even once this year, came into my class and asked me, with a conspiratorial expression, to call a Mr. Janos, who had phoned her to say that my wife, Judit, was worried about me. Finally a reason not to call, I thought happily. Finally I cannot be reached. I had finally escaped supervision. I was finally not participating in a game anymore.

Relieved, I went back to Munich.

6

As Günter and I were not get-
ting anywhere, I arranged to meet a famous Italian writer
who had translated Mandelstam into Italian and written
one of the best studies of the poet. He was to read from his
own works at the Academy that evening, but as he couldn't
read with a full stomach, I was to pick him up at three
o'clock at his hotel for a late lunch. That way he would have
time for a nap before the reading, which was to start at
eight. He did not need to sleep more than an hour, but it
did have to be an hour. He apparently felt so exhausted
from his flight (which could not have taken more than two
hours from Rome), that he was on the verge of canceling
the reading. As for me, after this brief phone call, with its
orgy of explanations, I, too, was exhausted, but I ascribed
the greater part of my fatigue to the fact that my knowledge of Italian had, as it were, dissolved in the course of the
call. I could hardly manage a sentence, and had uttered
more or less incoherent fragments into the receiver. I began
to sweat from embarrassment at having to impose my rudi-

mentary Italian (which only distantly, in its melody, recalled
the language) on such an important person, who was so
worn out by his long journey and so busy planning the
hours before the reading that he hadn't had the energy to
observe my embarrassment. Strange saint. Unlike his German colleagues, such as Günter (from whom I had learned
the details of his life), this man did not seem to be worried
about his career. He hated appearing in public, hated read-
ings, never went to award ceremonies where speeches were
delivered, and always turned down prizes. Although he was
over sixty, he still lived with his mother, in an apartment behind the Pantheon. She darned his socks, took his letters to
the post office, and answered the phone by expressing re-
gret that her son was not at home (though he would be
standing beside her all the while, trembling). They slept in
separate rooms, but left the doors open. I considered him
one of the most important humorists, an Italian Gogol,
while he considered himself a gifted tragedian, which, of
course, comes to the same thing in the end.

Naturally, I intended to persuade him to collaborate
with me on the Mandelstam project, and after my experience with the telephone call, I absolutely wanted to have
an interpreter with me at this first meeting. I had asked
Günter, of all people, for help—the very man who for
months had been trying to talk me out of the project altogether. But Günter did not show up. Günter suffered from
the illness, apparently common to many writers, of being
unreliable. In fact, sometimes that unreliability seemed to
be his only reliable source of inspiration. So I went alone
to the guest house where the great man was being put up,

a strangely shabby building downtown, which had no sign but was equipped with an intercom and a worn doorbell button that, when I touched it, promptly vanished into its plastic casing and could not be lured back but continued to howl like an animal in its den. After a few minutes the door opened, and out came several Japanese with instrument bags over their shoulders, covering their ears as they fled into the street like agile insects. I turned to the side and tried to appear casual as they passed. The door clicked shut and I began picking at the button again. On the other side I could hear the hysterical voice of Professor Bevilacqua, who was desperately trying to drown out the shrill sound of the bell. It's me, I shouted, I'm waiting down here for you. I shouted so loudly that the people working at the pharmacy next door came out and, along with housewives and chance passersby, slowly moved toward me, partly out of curiosity as to why a grown man was screaming at the wall, partly because they were annoyed that I was bringing business to a standstill. Clearly, shouting "It's me" was not appreciated. If I had shouted "It's not me," I probably would have got away with it. When the mass of people clustered around me heard the answering screams of the poet, which now sounded more like cries for help, they forced the door open without further ado, and a small van-guard, led by the pharmacist, stormed up the steps, where they found the same scene as below, only now in a more intimate guise: Professor Bevilacqua standing there, shout-ing into the intercom. He was still in his pajamas, or rather again in his pajamas, a fat man on the verge of collapse. As no one could find the fuse box, the pharmacist slammed a chair against the bell as hard as he could until it finally gave up the ghost. A profound silence followed, and the crowd dispersed. I waited outside until the professor and poet, who had forgotten our appointment and had wanted to lie down for an afternoon nap, finally appeared, to talk, I assumed, about Mandelstam. A bald man with a pear-shaped head, he had such a deeply pained look that I could do nothing but walk along beside him in silence. Every word seemed to reopen the wound my bell-ringing had inflicted on him. Forgive me...I began a sentence that, after a glance into his eyes, I did not complete. "This way" was the only reasonable construction I produced; as he seemed to understand it despite my miserable Italian, I repeated it as often as I could. This way. This way. This way. Eventually we stopped in front of a brewery, where a clanging din from within assaulted us. Cautiously, the professor approached the door, craning his head forward like a dog checking whether he would be allowed to enter; then he drew back as loudly laughing guests came out, whereupon he tried again, caught the scent of roast pork, and decided against it. This approach was repeated at various restaurants of different types, but whether they were Chinese, Italian, Portuguese, or Bavarian, he refrained from entering and let himself be driven further, accompanied by my cries of *This way,* which by now sounded absurd and no longer had anything to do with where we were going. At a certain point in this aimless walk, he stopped and asked where he could buy underwear. Underwear? Wasn't Italy the land of underwear, Rome the capital of underwear? I instantly thought of the countless boutiques for intimate apparel in the tangle of streets around the Spanish Steps, superbly appointed shops that looked like galleries and had nothing for sale but a few ridiculous pairs of undershorts in obscene colors. What did the Mandelstam scholar want? Undershorts, I repeated, and held both my hands in front of my crotch. The professor nodded. So I took him to a so-called haberdasher where the professor, as I observed through the window while I waited outside, was fitted with half a dozen pairs of Schiesser briefs, briefs with padding in front, and had them wrapped. A good investment of my Academy fee, he said happily as we resumed our restless downtown wandering. The time for our discussion of Mandelstam was running out when the professor stopped outside a small restaurant and decided, after much sniffing, to enter. A friendly black man, who introduced himself as James and, as we later learned, was from Uganda, offered us a table by the window, which we turned down for a table in the middle of the room. But when another guest arrived and sat down near us, we switched to a table by the door, which, because of the draft, had to be given up in favor of a tiny table by the restrooms. After James had also patiently replaced our hard chairs with upholstered ones, and the professor and I had traded places several times, first because the Mandelstam expert wanted to lend me his good ear, then because he did not want to look at a particular painting hanging innocently on the wall, we were finally able to examine the menu, which consisted largely of light Italian pasta dishes, but also featured *Tafelspitz* and several kinds of fish. James described it all to us in both German and English, with the persuasiveness peculiar to proud restaurateurs. After a long, embarrassing translation and a detailed discussion of what was actually a relatively short menu, the professor decided, with a worried look, on roast lamb with peas and potatoes (though without roast lamb, potatoes, or sauce), while I ordered spaghetti with garlic and oil. *Solo piselli?* I asked several times, but got no answer from the poet, who had sunk into a brooding silence. Professor Bevilacqua, his pear-shaped head hanging down onto his chest, appeared to have fallen asleep. Only when James had actually put a plate of peas, a hundred green peas, beside the glass of wine he had not touched, only then did the professor's plump body begin to move. With a limp hand, he reached for the fork and tried—vainly, if I may summarize all his efforts at ingesting food in one word—to skewer one pea after another, which the legumes evaded by springing away. Soon they were lying around the rim of his plate like a green wreath so that a diner who chanced to pass us might have thought the plate had been decorated in honor of the Italian who was looking at it with increasing unhappiness. Unwilling to appear impolite, I did not touch my spaghetti. Only when the professor managed to catch a few selected peas from the tablecloth with his fat fingers (and, in doing so, to mash them) and, after long examination, to stuff them into his mouth, only then, with my stomach starting to grumble, did I take a fork to my noodles. But no sooner had I started than the Italian, whom I had after all wanted to consult about a libretto for my Mandelstam opera, pursed his lips and, with gently twitching movements, spit the pea skins out. He then dragged the unruly skins across the plate until the green mass stuck to the porcelain. James, elated by the praise Bevilacqua had bestowed upon his cuisine, replaced his plate with the guest book, into which he had pasted a picture of the author, which he had clearly just cut out of the local evening paper. Now, I thought, the time is ripe for presenting my request. You should write opera to Mandelstam. That must have been roughly what the sentence sounded like, and it made the professor raise his pear-shaped head for a second from the guest book. It was not exactly a look of friendship and trust that he gave me; it was not even a look of contempt. What this revered writer's look expressed he summarized a moment later in one sentence: How can I write a libretto for an opera when I can't even read music? Whereupon he ordered a taxi, took elaborate leave of James, briefly nodded goodbye to me—See you at the reading—and disappeared with his package of underwear.

I called Günter to have him pick me up, but he was not at home. I called my apartment, and a disturbingly gloomy-sounding Janos answered. I hung up.

James brought me an espresso and questioned me about my Italian friend with the insistence peculiar to Central Africans. Afterward, we switched to grappa, and later to a cane liquor James's father produced in a secret brewery in Uganda; it had been delivered to his son through his country's embassy. Customers then flooded the restaurant and stuffed themselves on the meat Professor Bevilacqua had refused. About midnight, I finally reached Judit, who had attended the professor's reading with Günter and could not stop raving about it. Apparently he spoke perfect

German, and they had all gone to a Bavarian beer house. Günter was still in my apartment. They both came to pick me up, and with the help of the African host and his Swabian wife, they managed to get me into the backseat of my car. I then had a moment, for the first time that eventful day it seemed, to think about my opera, while I listened to the pair in the front seat, these two people who, during and after the reading by the Italian Mandelstam specialist, had clearly become lovers.

7

The thought of being declared insane sometimes warmed my heart. The life of a saint or a sinner, a cynic, moralist, or freethinker, a genuine article or a fool, a libertine in love with love, a mystery man or a hypocrite, a simpleton or an enigma, a forger, a split personality or an enthusiast, a swindler or an honest man, a suspect or at least a subversive, a party man or an enemy, a critic or a charlatan, an intellectual or a ne'er-do-well, a monster, a nonbeliever, or a nonbelieving believer, an invalid or just a curmudgeon, a mystic, an imitator, a bundle of energy, a blasphemer, an illusionist, a chosen one, a misanthrope, a magician, a victim, a shirker, a witness or, if possible, a witness of history, a seismograph (God forbid) or a creature of public opinion. Then at last this life packed with contradictory attributes, which, as an artist, I had been forced to lead, could be given up, and I would be free to live as the man I really was. A terrifying notion for identity fanatics. Better to remain an artist within one's own four walls.

8

One week before Judit's birthday, the actual preparations for her party began. The discussion had started long before: her dress, the accommodation of the guests, and the planning of events had dominated our conversation since my return from Madrid. As it had been years since I'd last celebrated my own birthday (since my mother's death, to be precise), I watched the changes in our household with apprehension and aversion. The fervor with which Judit pictured her relatives entering our festively decorated apartment made me suspect that they might stay. Forever, as the saying goes. Judit's nephews and nieces, as well as her aunts and uncles, would stay with us forever, and we would all be one big happy family. For almost twenty years, I had loved myself more or less steadfastly, and I had hoped to carry on that way until the end. But if it were up to Judit, I would love her family too, at least for a while, she said; forever, I suspected.

The actual incubation period—the time, that is, between the infection and the outbreak of the illness—began with the arrival of Uncle Sandor, a week before the great event. Uncle Sandor was a musicologist, and according to Judit, he was to help me recover; he alone would be able to restore the talent I had frittered away, so I would be able to create the masterpieces that she still thought me capable of producing in spite of all. I resisted his visit, of course. The idea of having to talk to a musicologist from the Lukács school about my Mandelstam opera (which by then had come to be called the Mandelstam project, as if its failure were preordained), was repugnant to me not because I was sitting there empty-handed, with a few sketches and vague ideas, but because I suspected that her uncle, too, might belong to the syndicate Judit had assembled exclusively to block my project. I had found a few of his articles in anthologies from the sixties. The way they scraped together just enough material to justify a theory that turned living arbitrariness into embalmed pedantry exuded a suffocating boredom and left me cold. Schooled in Marxism, Uncle Sandor began with statistics, with numerical relationships (salaries, surplus value, profits) instead of with what music required; and from the abstract numbers he calculated a morality, an aesthetics, and a metaphysics, if that term can even be justified. This is the way to understand the music of the eighteenth century, he would conclude cheerfully, this is the way to listen to music. When I tried to explain her uncle's lack of imagination to Judit, she always gave the same answer. Those essays are from the old days; to be published that was how they had to be written. Her uncle was completely different now, much deeper, wiser, more inspired; I would be astonished by the sure hand with

which he would lead me out of my darkness. It was sense-
less to attempt to counter such certainty, so I surrendered
to the rather unpleasant thought of having to spend a
week working on the Mandelstam opera alongside my
silent friend Janos and a Hungarian musicologist.

Uncle Sandor, the early harbinger of the expected clan,
was in fact quite different from the way Judit had described
him. First of all, he was a giant, a monster with a gnome's
long beard; in fact, he was so unnaturally tall that when he
sat and talked he would instinctively try to make himself
smaller by slowly sliding his bottom forward on the cush-
ion until his head touched the back of the chair, which
meant he was almost reclining, his long legs rising up like
a barrier in front of him and covering his meager body. In
this anything but comfortable position, he murmured to
the ceiling in a state of inexorable melancholy, each sentence an appendage to a small cloud of tobacco smoke.
Uncle Sandor, who was about my age but had the air of a
very old man, was lost without his pipe. Immediately upon
arrival, he deposited a pipe at every strategically important
point in the apartment, and he always kept one burning
while the next was being filled. Even at lunch—he ate virtually nothing because of a stomach ailment—he would
unabashedly smoke his nasty-smelling tobacco and send
pungent clouds drifting over the food. I once asked if he
could take a brief break from smoking during dessert so
Judit and I could eat our sugared strawberries without
coughing; in the silence that followed my suggestion, he put
the angrily crackling pipe on the table, without a thought
for the red-hot embers that soon freckled and ruined the

cloth, then fished a cigar stub from his vest pocket and lit up with no sign of guilt. While I stared at him aghast— such innocent foulness seemed immoderate to me—he continued his lecture unmoved. We have been released into plurality, he said, sending the words in pursuit of the gray clouds; a new age of the arts will dawn, for we no longer need the truth espoused by Lukács.

Lukács was present in each of his sentences. In every other one he was mentioned by name, and the lectures often culminated in the phrase: This evening, even I no longer really understand what Lukács thought.

The sad refutation of Lukács and the smoke of the pipe: Uncle Sandor's life went back and forth between those two poles. Reaching for his pipe was his only living gesture; the rest was a circus performance he kept finding or borrowing new phrases for, like the "braggadocio of beauty" that he evoked whenever anything seemed flat to him "in our starless night that dreams of morning, when things and forms will be visible again. Morning air is blowing into the dusty room, and the dawn of a new world is touching the broken brows of those who have learned, in the darkness, to believe in a new world—which does not exist, of course."

It was strange how Uncle Sandor, whom I secretly called the mossback, because the few teeth left in his mouth were covered by a thick, greenish layer of scum, how Uncle Sandor brought a vocabulary into our everyday life that was not part of Judit's own rather practical, goal-oriented usage. By then I was already responding to Judit's suspicious questions and growing demands in a defensive way, and I was afraid that such an elaborate manner of speaking would only heighten the domestic confusion she called order. Uncle Sandor, born in 1941 to Jewish parents under wretched conditions in Budapest, had created, in part through his extensive reading and in part through forcibly acquired Marxist terminology, an unfamiliar, foreign, occasionally even homely language that infiltrated our exchanges, which had already been reduced to demands and reluctant replies. I often wondered whether Judit understood her uncle's meandering tirades, in which the defetishizing mission of art was effortlessly related to the formless, self-sufficient diversity of the spirit that inspired it, and that, in turn, to the rise of the bourgeoisie and the decline of the feudal class, until I had to admit that even I was simply listening to his words without understanding what he was talking about. And then suddenly I would come back to earth amid clouds of smoke at the mention of Stalin, the gifted Marxist theoretician, whose comments on the "conscious," "systematic" side of Casanova's love affairs would appear, only to be supplanted, without any apparent transition, by the mossback's ruminations on the function of the veil, whose folds created confusion because they were the already wrinkled reflection of the body they covered. These monumental structures of speech had no girders, no bridges or passages, no relay stations that could have given the steadily flowing narration a particular order. This learned man had lost them. So he staggered through libraries, creeping among the words with his smoking pipe, picking up something here or there and carrying it around with him for a while only to put it down again somewhere else, astonished by the effects generated by such a scattershot method, which was of course doomed to oblivion. He had abandoned Marxism for the open desert of text, which was no longer limited by any historical-philosophical horizon, and now all he had to hold on to was his pipe. And his life story. It was one of those stories that epitomized the century. A story that took place in New York, where his father's brother had been a famous lawyer and jazz aficionado, but also in Moscow, where his mother had worked for the Comintern. Opera houses in Paris and Berlin played as central a role in this story as smoke-filled back rooms in Palestine, where his uncle Tibor ran a Zionist office. The mossback's father had worked for the Jewish newspaper *Vj Kelet* and had negotiated until the end—and without any hope of success—with Hermann Krumey, Eichmann's deputy in Budapest. The stories ended where all such stories end: in Auschwitz. Informers betrayed the family and robbed them of their last pengö before they were murdered. Only Uncle Sandor, the giant former musicologist who was now the family historian, had survived.

After our first conversation, it was abundantly clear that Uncle Sandor would be no good as a cicerone. Subjected to his teaching method, I would have to give up composing sooner or later, so it was crucial to keep him away from me. Fortunately, no tactful diplomacy was necessary—the uncle, who still had the silent Janos to listen to his speeches when I had had enough, had another passion besides his own philosophical discourse: television. Wearing his suit and vest, he would lie in front of the tube in his inimitable posture, mumbling and brushing the crumbs from his mighty gray beard while hopping tirelessly from program to program. While Judit and I were busy making birthday preparations and rearranging the apartment, which meant carrying tables, chests of drawers, and boxes of books between Sandor and the television set, the Uncle could not be distracted. I had a suspicion that German television stations, especially private German television stations, were a concrete replacement for his collapsed world view; in that little rectangle, the things that were falling apart were put together again to form an order life no longer provided. Television was the night he safely walked through, the talking library he reached into at random for inspiration. He was the most old-fashioned modernist I have ever encountered, and he was staggeringly lazy. We worked, and he watched television.

At the end of the week, the apartment looked the way Judit wanted it to. The Polish cleaning lady, who had started out allied with me against change (which included a reordering of the pictures), had switched to Judit's side; now the two of them discussed all the major issues, such as turning my study into a bedroom for Aunt Julia, in Russian. I found myself in a polyglot family that had demoted me to the role of helper. With the arrival of the aunt and her escort, a Romanian doctor, my days in the apartment were numbered. The uncle in the living room, Janos in the guest room, the Romanian doctor in the bathroom with the door open and his pants down (giving himself an insulin shot), the aunt in the piano room where, to Judit's delight, she practiced Bartók's "Fourteen Bagatelles," Judit herself in the kitchen preparing baked goods and fruit preserves with her girlfriends from the conservatory, and in my own room an entire Hungarian family of dubious origin, who, not having any other place to stay, had simply occupied my bed. No one seemed to know how those four people were related to Judit's family, and as they did not socialize with anyone, there was no way to find out. Sometimes the children could be heard crying, while the father screamed at them to be quiet because he had to work, and the mother could occasionally be heard humming Bartók's Hungarian peasant dances.

As a result, I had no choice but to move into Judit's studio—the garret above the apartment that had once been my studio—with the few possessions I could still find. Despite the opportunity to work again, I had reservations about the move. Though anyone who saw us together had to suspect that ours was not the conventional relationship between an old family friend and a girlfriend's daughter, at least before now the evidence of our complicity had been kept under wraps. With the move from my domain into hers, everything became clear, and I could imagine the tongues wagging below.

Don't be so small-minded, said Judit, as we sat on her bed with a bottle of champagne on the eve of her birthday; everyone know we're lovers. Everyone but you. Then she fell back on the bed, laughing, and I cautiously lay down beside her, feeling that the entire Hungarian nation was watching me do so.

Thank God I woke up at my usual hour and could think about our situation before Judit's mother arrived. I had to be able to provide an explanation. I could not just get out of bed and thank her for kindly sending me her daughter. But what could I say? I glanced furtively at the sleeping Judit, that sibylline creature, with her thin neck and the small golden cross that encircled it. If I said nothing, but only silently pointed at Judit, what would she say? To prevent the worst wouldn't I have to speak first? The terrible suspicion surged over me that Judit might announce our engagement in front of the whole family; yes, suddenly I was absolutely sure that all the energy she was investing, the insistence with which she had demanded that even her most distant relatives be present, could only lead to a marriage announcement. Why else would all the paupers we were expecting have exchanged their hard-earned money for deutsch marks? Judit needed witnesses. She wanted to make a show out of a formless affair, with half of Hungary acting as extras, listening while I gave my extorted "I do" in the presence of the mother of the bride. And while Judit stretched luxuriously in her sleep, which made the cross on her neck slide down a little, I wondered why I, of all people, had been the chosen one. In the past few weeks, she had taken to inviting students from the Academy over. They would sit around my kitchen table and more or less openly criticize my music, as if she had asked them beforehand to humiliate me in as friendly a way as possible. One student in particular, who was studying composition with a friend of mine at the Academy, made brazen remarks that I let go so as not to demean myself in front of Judit, who had probably put him up to it. He talked about my works as though even I must find them no longer acceptable. Surely you must have already

written off your piano pieces? he asked me affably. Surely
today you no longer want your songs performed? And although I would not have objected to having my piano
pieces and songs broadcast on every radio station around
the world, I reacted as if I had been found out and even
claimed that these pieces meant little to me in the context
of my oeuvre. There was no argument. To that bright boy,
to that intelligent asshole who babbled about theory while
pseudoscientific jargon dribbled from his mouth, to that
unpleasant person it was clear I had got on the wrong boat.
And when, in her underhanded way, and seemingly in all
innocence, Judit told the group about my Mandelstam
project, the young man almost died laughing. That can't
be true, he gasped over his goulash; you have to rethink
that one. And then he vanished again into a thick cloud of
problem content and diagnostic material, a haze of tran-
scendental acoustics and chronocritical calculations of loss,
and then went on to the deadly power of musical symbols,
which he hoped would keep me from assaulting Mandelstam. I didn't have a single note on paper, of course. All
dry runs, the leaps of an imagination sullied by theory and
trying to bridge an essentially shallow abyss. My stubborn
silence in the face of such frothy eloquence led Judit to re-
tire to her studio with the sensitive philosopher, where, on
the basis of a piece he had written for cello, they were
going to discuss the "significance of symbolic experience,"
as the young man put it. They had probably fallen into the
very same bed I was now lying in, for when I came up and
rang the bell an hour later, just before midnight, the door
was not opened for me, although, standing still, holding

my breath, I could hear clearly identifiable sounds coming from the room, and they were not those of a cello.

Why didn't she marry that know-it-all Laszlo, son of now wealthy Hungarian immigrants from 1956, who had made their money in the fur trade? The deconstruction specialist and the woman looking for truth—an ideal pair, as I saw it. Janos or Laszlo? It should be one of the two.

Judit had now extricated her leg from the sheet and displayed it, oddly twisted, on the bedspread. It looked as if it were on an operating table, neatly severed from the rest of the body, the toes pointing up. On her ankle, she had a thin golden chain I had not seen her wear before. Gently, so as not to wake her, I bent over to look at it more closely. From the narrow, finely wrought gold threads, whose links fit together in a serrated shape, came such an uncanny fascination that I finally reached out my hand and touched the little chain. Somebody before me had tried to enchain this body, and with a movement at once angry and ludicrous, I tore the sheet from the sleeping girl.

The birthday girl woke up. But not in her usual way, struggling through a thicket of waning dreams into the morning—she woke up instantly. And as if she had seen through me, she pulled up her legs while opening her arms, into which I let myself fall. The first well-wisher. In this strange, uncomfortable position, I forgot to ask about the source of the chain, though I could feel it with my foot, while my mouth, gasping for breath, ended up on the golden cross, which I grabbed with my teeth and held between my lips until I was finally released. Breakfast had to be readied for the family waiting below, so Judit pushed me

away, leaped out of bed, and disappeared into the bathroom, where she turned on all the faucets and, singing
loudly, began her morning toilette.

I stayed in bed. Rarely in my life had I felt so miserable
and superfluous. Torn by guilt, jealousy, and a healthy dose
of self-hatred, I couldn't imagine ever getting out of bed
again. At such moments, for a fraction of a second, most
people have a sense of how the world fits together, but all
I felt was a coarse fatigue that crushed any hint of well-
being. I turned to stone. At first, I couldn't move my legs,
then my head stopped obeying commands. Finally, my
arms were out of commission. Somewhere inside me was
an idea that could have helped me escape this trap, but I
couldn't find it. When Judit came out of the bathroom,
naked but for a towel on her head, she must have intu-
itively sensed my condition, for while she was getting
dressed with no sign of emotion, she said with feigned
concern: my poor stone, my poor darling stone, thrown
into bed and left lying there forever.

I must have actually fallen asleep again, for when I
woke after endless wandering through a cemetery whose
tombstones were made of books, a group of people was
standing around the bed. Except for Judit, I recognized
only Uncle Sandor, pipe in his mouth, breakfast tray in his
hands. A bacchanalia of ghosts, a dance of death. Fearfully, I pulled the sheet up to my neck, hoping that this
scene, too, was nothing more than a sequence in my
dream. But all too soon I realized what was what, as Judit
took the tray from her uncle with crafty aplomb, put it on
my belly, and said: Enjoy your breakfast, darling stone.

Whereupon the group was taken on a tour of the studio. Then the door slammed. They had left, and Judit had not found it necessary to check on the patient. The party had started without me.

O loam-and-life! O century's demise!
To him alone it will confide, I fear,
your sense, in whom there was a helpless smile—
the man who lost himself, the heir.

9

When I came downstairs in the early afternoon, the apartment was packed. The exact number of guests could not be established because they were spread out in every room. Judit's fellow students were serving coffee, tea, and cake; Janos's silence was full of import; two aunts from Debrecen were cleaning up; the family residing in my bedroom were doing the dishes; Maria's nephew was shuffling from room to room with a bottle and a tray of schnapps glasses; Judit wandered among all the groups, laughing and chatting, sitting down only to leap up again. She was the center of attention and seemed to have even the most remote provinces firmly in her grasp. In my apartment, her word was law. I felt like a dethroned king, still acknowledged and shyly greeted but essentially irrelevant. I suspected they were ridiculing me behind my back, because sometimes I'd approach a group, and the conversation would terminate abruptly, only to start again the minute I left. In Judit's empire, Hungarian was spoken. German was allowed, but only when it was necessary.

In my barbarically redone study, Uncle Sandor was lying in a chair, surrounded by smirking young people, as with a sorrowful expression he shared anecdotes from the time when people still believed in musical truth. The mossback spat out one stale joke after another from his inexhaustible memory, invariably expressed in a language that must have sounded like Latin to his audience: the utopia of reconciliation; the promise of truth; the historical necessity of music as a discipline. Occasionally he added, as if apologizing: if such an expression can still be used today. It could. But when I joined the group, because the chatter in the other reaches of the apartment bored me and also because I could at least hope to understand some of the talk here, the conversation almost immediately lost its informality. Because I was daring enough to still put notes on paper, and because I was so rash as to claim that I could imagine a tonal masterpiece in this day and age, and because I was stupid enough to put forward the idea that one should be pleased when a work responds to social reality and that this reality was clearly shaped more by the electronic media than by the best chamber music, a cry of feigned indignation ran through the room. In an instant the converted Marxist had joined forces with the fanatical deconstructionists to read me the riot act, which culminated in the conclusion that I was basically a musical fascist. Whoever had not comprehended the explosion of musical works, indeed of the Western artwork as such, brought about by Cage and his successors was not in a position to "envisage" a different music, let alone to compose. And so on and so on. In my distress, which was now not only an expression of indisposition but also something rising from deeper layers, I grabbed one of the few books still visible among the decorations in my room, a collection of Schönberg's writings, and read, my voice cracking and my hand raised to stop the irresponsible tittering once and for all, his preface to Webern's "Six Bagatelles":

"These pieces can only be understood by someone who has faith that, through notes, something that can only be said with notes can be expressed. They can withstand critique no better than this or any other faith. If faith can move mountains, lack of faith cannot let them exist. Faith is impotent against such impotence. Now, does the musician know how to play these pieces, the listener know how to accept them? Can faithful players and listeners fail to give themselves to each other? But what should one do with the heathen? Fire and sword can make them quiet, but only the faithful can be spellbound."

I slammed the book shut so hard that a thick cloud of smoke stirred from Uncle Sandor's pipe; then, in an act of pure drama, I threw the book into a corner. So, the gesture seemed to suggest, think about that for a while. And with that, I left the group.

It was past five o'clock, and it was starting to rain. I sat down at the kitchen table, which was now covered with bowls full of noodles. The friendly Hungarians greeted me and made room for me to rest my elbows on the table. A glass of wine appeared in front of me. Somewhere in the house, a party was going on; at any rate, well-dressed people kept drifting in and out.

Enveloped by the kitchen sounds and the pelting rain outside the open window, but still inwardly excited about my little performance, I was in an odd mood: half rebellious, half at a loss. One question, especially, haunted me and could not be silenced: had I found Judit as one finds an object (a beautiful object, of course) that one picks up because one cannot leave it lying there? My apartment was full of such sacred objects, which on the surface may have seemed to be good only for gathering dust, but which had a meaning for me. Sometimes the meaning faded, and they ended up in the garbage; other times they changed their meaning and rose in the hierarchy of my attention. They reminded me of moments in my life that changed as my attention changed, and not always for the better. To celebrate a small collection of stones I had gathered in Sardinia years ago, I once composed a piece that imitated the sounds of waves rolling over pebbles. It had its premiere in Hannover in a large studio with too much brass, and a critic suggested I use the piece for an episode in my detective series; it would play better there than on the concert stage. (He had, by the way, not noticed that I had used and varied a theme by Saint-Saëns.) But can one find people?

Or had I met her as one unexpectedly meets people who suddenly rob one of reason, when one's will has fallen asleep or else has dried up? I can think of several such instances in my life. My first wife, Helga, crossed my path in a Berlin dive, at a time when my life was as dark as it had ever been. When I saw her sitting there with someone a few tables away, cocooned in an agitated restlessness, I somehow knew I would meet her, with all the unavoidable consequences. That inner certainty had no sooner crept over me, despite my depression, when a friend walked into the bar. He first said hello to me, then went to the table of my future wife and waved me over to them. I succeeded in forcing the woman's companion to leave in no time, and then I put the closeness of unfamiliarity into practice. You've met me; now we must act, I insisted; no argument can convince me otherwise. All my decrepitude suddenly fell from me like an old skin. We were married three weeks later.

But Judit? We had not met like that, not at all.

So had she been sent to me? By Maria? Did Maria have a reason to send her daughter to me? In order not to be grounded by false suspicions and the fog of my own sad story, I thought again of the fateful day we met. For if Judit is merely performing a disgraceful mission, then, young as she is, she will someday give herself away. She won't hold out, I thought; despite the apparently limitless energy of her youth, a girl of twenty-three will make a mistake that will drive her out of the fortified castle of her mission into the labyrinth of her feelings, and she will only find her way out with outside help, with my help. I had to take up the fight against this creature in order not to fall prey to her magic. Above all, I had to come down from the height of my assumed superiority and fearlessly bet everything on one number. But on which number? I longed for Maria, because I hoped her arrival would clarify matters. If, as was uncertain but not impossible, I fell in love with Judit's mother again, her daughter would have to come clean. Love would strip suspicion of its power. But why in the world should Judit love me?

While playing with a few mussel-shaped noodles that had not been boiled to death, I ran through the various constellations of suspicion, betrayal, and love. Just as I was putting one piece of pasta on top of another, Judit came into the kitchen and startled me out of my brooding with hectic gestures. What kind of oblivious host are you, she cried; it's the birthday of the one person dearer to you than anyone else in the world, and you're sitting here in the kitchen, playing with noodles. Then she took my head in her hands and kissed my brow, melting my resolution to take up the fight. I surrendered, stood up, and followed her into the mass of guests, which had grown even thicker, in order to introduce myself and ask people how they were.

I got into a conversation with an old doctor who had been a friend of Judit's grandfather in Budapest. He had practiced first in Italy and later in England, and was now living in Munich, where he had been writing his memoirs for years. He was married to a woman forty years his junior. We live very similar lives, he said cheerfully. Poor fool, I thought. He invited me to visit him, and I accepted, though I knew I would never look him up voluntarily. I never go into strangers' apartments unless I am forced to. My second wife had enjoyed "having people over," which forced me to socialize with concert managers and program directors, doctors and businessmen's wives, race-horse owners and plastic surgeons, all of them interested in me as a composer of music for television, but never seen at the few concerts where my serious music was performed. These people were only interested in themselves, and attending opera festivals, summer piano series, and benefit concerts with untalented Third World violinists were just a pretext to meet people one could have over, to be had over by them in turn. Many of them went so far as to announce their parties in the newspaper, and after the gossip column reported that I had been seen at the Duchess of Saxony-Weimar's with the car dealer Peter Brunnthaler, whose photo was in the newspaper every day, I refused to go out ever again. From then on, my second wife went to the dinners and cocktails and receptions alone, and one could read about how happy and carefree she looked at so-and-so's side. Even today, she occasionally makes an appearance in the tabloids, because her new husband, a plastic surgeon, is responsible for the cloned zombies whose houses she frequents. Often I don't recognize her, but sometimes a vague memory stirs in me. Yes, I was once married to her. Yes, she now lives with a plastic surgeon. Yes, I think I once loved her. No, I don't love her anymore.

The Hungarian doctor gave me his card, which I carefully slid into my wallet. See you soon, I said to him. Then Judit led me to the next cluster, in the middle of which sat a Hungarian painter who had lived in Munich since 1958 and had become a professor at the local art school. I had to force myself to listen as this gnome, spurred on by my presence, laboriously recited his wise sayings. His loud, nasal voice was even more disgusting to me than the words it carried. Poor students, I whispered to myself; the fiasco will not be long in coming.

After an agonizing tour of the party, we again landed in my former study, where the aestheticians, who had been provided with food in the meantime, were still talking about the aporias of Modernism, though now with their mouths full.

That was enough. I no longer had any reason to stay in my apartment. With the excuse that I had to go to the toilet, I left the room and the party crowd, got a jacket from the top floor, and set out on a walk along the Isar, where I hoped at this hour of the evening to be left in peace.

10

The rain had driven people inside. Except for a bicyclist loudly bellowing Ravel's *Bolero* into the downpour, I saw nobody as I walked downstream along Thomas Mann Weg. I wanted to go to the dam and head back on the other side of the English Garden, a brisk two-hour walk. In the highway underpass lay a bicycle with two flat tires. There was always a musty smell at that spot, so it was always a relief to have that twenty-meter stretch behind me. A pigeon up in the struts released droppings right at my feet; that was lucky, I thought, if you had been one step ahead, it would have shat in your face. I stepped up my pace. A gust of wind shook drops from the trees, and I raised my face to receive them.

Ever since Judit had slipped into my life, whether she had been sent or I had met or found her, I had stopped going for walks down this path. In a certain sense, she *had* made my life richer, of course; her youth had opened my eyes to things that, for fear of being distracted, I no longer paid attention to. But she had also trapped me, taken the air out of my sails, cut off my whims with a stream of questions. When I wanted to set out alone on one of my walks, I was asked whether I had got any work done, and when I didn't answer, but silently put on my coat, she asked whether I couldn't help her with one thing or another, and when I responded by asking whether the thing couldn't be dealt with later, she would say that I only thought about myself and didn't care one iota about her. So I would take off my coat and listen to her play the cello, which she would have practiced without me anyway, and if I dared to criticize her playing, she would claim, laughing, that it was astonishing how little I, a musician, knew about the cello. I was only supposed to be present and experience her: her playing, her food, her family, her ideas, her appearance, even her drawing, which she was the first to admit was terrible. Soon she would make me lose pleasure in my own work. For while she had nothing against my going into the studio for three days every two weeks to earn a lot of money at the mixing board, her carping about my serious composition was becoming harsher and harsher. By this time she had "worked through" my complete oeuvre and made judgments about it that she was not qualified to make, expressing them with a disarming impudence. Here and there she found "the beginning of something interesting"; sometimes she praised a passage in a piece that, unfortunately, had otherwise failed; and one day she came to me with the happy news that the central work of my entire canon was the song I had dedicated to her mother, even though it was quite transparently inspired by Hanns Eisler, if not modeled on or even stolen from him. But there's something about it you can be proud of, she acknowledged. It has the aroma of its time.

It was written the year you were born, Judit, in Berlin; how can you know what the aroma of that time was? And by the way, that time had many things, but certainly not an aroma. Smell, taste, stench, whatever you like—but not an aroma. However, after an hour of insane argument, that time *had* an aroma, and my song, which was actually only tolerable when Maria sang it as she had sung it then, was that aroma's most precise musical expression. I could confidently discard the rest.

I had never claimed to be one of the great masters of my generation. I was always embarrassed by praise, especially at prize ceremonies; when, with the best intentions, majestic comparisons are made. When, in my youth, I received the Regensburg Grant for Young Talent, I sat beside the winner of the main prize, a hard-of-hearing wood sculptor with rough hands that stuck out of the white cuffs of his coarse jacket like moles. I repeated the mayor's speech about me, which was teeming with great names, into his ear. You are a student of Schönberg's? he shouted into the paralyzed hall, well done at your age; as for me, I worked the wood without guidance. And while the mayor, undeterred, tried to get to the end of the speech his cultural representative had written for him, the sculptor, equally undeterred, continued to express his pleasure at being allowed to sit beside a student of Schönberg's, until the hall was filled with laughter louder than any heard in Regensburg since the Middle Ages.

But despite reservations about comparing my own works to those of others, some work had emerged that I could be proud of, and it surely would have received more recognition if I had not resisted becoming a part of the outrageous swindle involved in the promotion of culture. That very day, I read in the paper that a former film director had sat on a pile of manure in a horse stall in Weimar and read Nietzsche out loud. Surely an event. Even I would have made the paper if I had begun a reading from *Beyond Good and Evil* by ringing a couple of cowbells. But I don't want to sit on horseshit and ring in Nietzsche with cowbells. I have never wanted to, and I still don't want to.

I was so busy screaming a defiant "I don't want to" into the gleaming curtain of rain at the dam that I didn't see the straggly-haired woman standing there until she turned toward me. What don't you want? she asked in a piping voice that barely penetrated the heavy downpour.

I don't want to compose under certain conditions anymore, I answered truthfully.

And what do you want to do instead? the woman asked. If only I knew. What does someone like me want to do?

Compose, I said. I want to compose, but only for myself from now on.

Surely one doesn't compose just for oneself, said the woman.

And what are you doing here? I asked. She did not answer, just stared into space.

Come, I said, if you keep standing here all alone in the rain, you'll lose all desire to live and throw yourself in. People are forever throwing themselves in from this spot. And dying, because the water's shallow. Leaving people behind who don't know what to do either, so they marry, get a job, and die someday. Always with the photograph of a former lover in their pockets, right behind the last hundred-mark bill. Why don't we go to the Aumeister, have a schnapps together, and talk about what we don't want to do under any circumstances in the future?

She hesitated, but then came along. I spoke to her as if I were wound up, although I was not at all sure whether that would bring her closer to suicide or take her farther away from it. At the Aumeister, we were each served a double schnapps, which we had to drink standing up beside the overflowing umbrella stands in the front room. When she finally revealed her name to me, I had to laugh out loud: Maria. A completely soaked Maria, a dripping poodle to whom I, of all people, was lecturing that one has to want to do something in life in order to no longer want anything. We drank another schnapps to that. Later, I made sure she really did enter her apartment on Kaiserstrasse. Standing at the lit window, she waved to me. I was happy. I had written her name and telephone number on the back of the Hungarian doctor's card. We'll meet again, if you like, she had said. We'll meet again.

I returned around eleven o'clock, a happy, dripping man, to the middle of the Hungarian colony. My reception was anything but friendly; the voices were low as I stood in the doorway. The well-wishers, many already drunk and red in the face, moved to the side, creating a path at the end of which, like an icon, stood Maria and Judit, the mother's hand on the innocent daughter's shoulder. They gazed grimly at the sinner.

II

There was a time when it was considered good form for a young musician to take part in music festivals in the Warsaw Pact countries. Such gatherings contributed to understanding between peoples. One really did get to know a lot of participants from different countries, listening to music together, eating and drinking through the night, and finally exchanging addresses.

From the mid sixties on, I always enjoyed going to Warsaw. The Polish musicians were more intellectually curious than my Western colleagues. And my Western colleagues were more tolerable in Warsaw or Krakow than in Cologne or Donaueschingen. More was at stake. For the three or four days we spent every year in Warsaw during Youth Music Week, the city belonged to us. People listened to us, they wanted to listen to us. We sat until closing time in smoke-filled bars, then talked until dawn in the public squares. Anything said about modern music that sounded forced or pretentious in Germany dissolved in the Polish nights: suddenly the issue was music again, not music and society. In Warsaw and Krakow, there were no points to be scored by claiming one wanted to blow up the opera houses, nor did roping workers into choirs go down well in Poland. Polish workers did not want to sing. German workers listened to folk music and pop songs, preferably by Mireille Mathieu and Vicky Leandros, then they would sing or hum along. But by then German workers were no longer real workers, while Polish workers, who were still real workers, or so my friends thought, were not yet lost to art. But even Polish workers, depressingly enough, were not interested in Modernism, and especially not in modern music. My friends' reaction to this lack of interest was intriguing. Those who wanted to advance their idea of a socialist music everywhere sooner or later landed in the arms of the secret police, who had their hands full trying both to reinforce these naive notions and to get their advocates out of the country as quickly as possible, before the seeds of their idealistic absurdities could sprout; in contrast, everyone else conformed in one way or another. One way was to become a worshipper of both avant-garde music and socialism, but separately and for separate audiences, so as not to betray either party. Another possibility, which was also of interest to the secret police, was to despise both the capitalist and the socialist music systems. A West German musician invited to perform in Warsaw or Krakow, but who refused to play his music or even to have it played by others, had to arouse suspicion. The upshot of all this was that there was always somebody sitting at the table at our exuberant sessions and listening closely, somebody nobody knew. Sometimes it was a friend from the GDR who recorded our discussions, and occasionally there was even someone from the West who wanted to earn a bit from the GDR on the side. Whenever one of us was missing the next time we got together, in Budapest or Prague or East Berlin, it was obvious that someone had squealed, but as it could not be any of those who were present, we continued to be careless in what we said.

I liked going to Budapest best of all. In Budapest, people were less formal than in other Eastern bloc countries. When the young Western pedants put their theories on display there, they were met with bitter irony. Our French colleagues, in particular, were made to suffer. No matter how much effort they invested in harmonizing electronic music with the demands of dialectical materialism, their sole reward would always be laughter. One brief but hearty laugh. How could one be such a fool! Bourgeois society, the sole condition worth striving for as far as most of my Hungarian friends were concerned, had to be overcome so that bourgeois music could develop its revolutionary potential. Of course, most of the Hungarians I met came from aristocratic or upper-middle-class families, and their appearance and manner reflected something of that past. The conspirators were missing, as were the commissars, so the shrillness of argument vanished and our meetings often seemed more like rehearsals. We were rehearsing our lives. In these performances, the French played the educated scoundrels and the Germans the revolutionary fools, while the rest had to make do with roles as extras. The Hungarians made the music.

Among the Hungarian composers, there was one I felt especially drawn to. I met him in Leipzig at the house of a positively charismatic music historian who had written a standard work on Eisler. Everybody who wanted to know anything about Eisler came by at some point to the cave of books that Helmut lived in. Helmut was a man of dwarfish stature, who would always leap up just when a discussion threatened to become interminable and, in his warbling voice, sing us a song by Eisler. He *was* Eisler. And since all revolutionary composers at that time had to take Eisler into account because he had left behind, along with his music, a number of essays on the delicate problems of communication, this young Hungarian composer also turned up in Helmut's apartment. We became friends at once. He spoke fabulous German, of course. Not just because all Hungarian composers speak German (along with many other languages), but because he came from a Jewish German-Hungarian family that, in a kind of crash course, had taught this last surviving heir pretty much everything the rest of us could never teach ourselves, not in a very long lifetime. He had read everything and remembered everything. Pushkin and Rilke, the history of philosophy and of music, the natural sciences and the occult sciences, Marx and Freud. He had the bulk of the piano literature in his head, and not just the traditional part. And as he was also incapable of leaving a half-empty bottle alone, he had grown accustomed to a rather peculiar kind of sociability. This man, tall as a tree and thin as a rail, would sit with us at a table for hours without saying a word. Cloaked in an aura of melancholy and absentmindedness, he stared into space—smoking, occasionally humming a few bars that happened to be going through his head, sighing, massaging his nicotine-stained fingers—and said nothing. He would remain silent until someone tugged at his sleeve and asked him for some information, which he would provide forthwith, thoroughly and cheerfully, whether it concerned Schubert, the Talmud, or Hungarian history. Then, almost at once, he would re-enter his silence, which some interpreted as shyness, others as lack of self-confidence, but most as a special form of mild arrogance. His name was Janos. As a youth, he had been a party member, but he had soon left party politics, then given up a much sought after lectureship at the conservatory. He also refused a post he had been offered as a music editor. At thirty, he had produced more than most of us— short pieces for the most part, which Western radio stations loved to play. He lived off of that. And somehow he lived better than all of his colleagues of the same age in Hungary. Beyond that, he always managed to get a visa, so he showed up at all the major contemporary-music festivals in the West as well, a first-class listener who would sit silently after a concert, until he was asked a question. With such behavior, it did not take long for the rumor to spread that he was a spy who would one day turn us all in. A German theoretician, a comrade from Munich whose pedantic way of tracking down the class struggle in music history turned all our seminar participants against him, bruited about his dubious conjectures concerning Janos, not omitting the familiar anti-Semitic insinuations. Suddenly, the gentle young man was a cunning spy, sitting at our table and taking note of everything on a secret mission for the party, in order to use it against us. Then it was my turn to denounce the denouncer, as a GDR agent, and I succeeded in discrediting him, aided by the inept comrade's own unpopularity. But a shadow still clung to my friend Janos, a shadow of mistrust and suspicion, which haunts him even today.

I, for one, profited from Janos's friendship. As he stayed with me for weeks at a time, I had ample opportunity to enjoy his generosity and magnanimity. He helped me with everything. He was also the one who removed the straitjacket of materialist philosophy from me—a long, painful process.

His mother's family had been murdered in the German concentration camps; his father, a famous Communist, died in a work camp in the "fatherland of the world proletariat." He left behind thirty-five letters that comprised an anthology of hunger and interrogations, of vitamin deficiency and of revolutionary fervor, a documentation of the attempt to obliterate his individuality, describing depression, melancholy, anxiety, and longing, as well as the friendship of two German comrades who died miserably right before his eyes. Janos knew those letters by heart, word for word, and whenever one of our Communist colleagues from Cologne or Paris or Milan thought it necessary to reproach someone for not being orthodox enough, Janos would mumble a passage from the letters describing his father's suffering. He was always the first to see through the grimace that invariably accompanied the party line.

He was the one who drew me to Budapest at every opportunity. And it was through him that I met Maria.

12

When, having been back home for a week, utterly exhausted, I read the musicians' names jotted down on crumpled scraps of paper that fell out of my pockets like confetti, it was virtually impossible to picture the faces that matched them. There were not only Slovakian folk-dance groups, Slovenian jazz musicians, Russian violinists, and Azerbaijani flutists, but also young Communist musicians from Cuba, Paris, and the Ivory Coast, and they all had names, addresses, questions, and hopes. And just when I had finally recovered from all the speeches—and the alcoholic excesses that helped me get through the speeches—and just when I had finally sat down again at my desk to start working, letters would begin to arrive, recalling conversations and promises. So I would go in search of sheet music, look for rare records, and purchase books, which had to be mailed to every conceivable country, and when that tiresome and expensive task was finally done—a task that distracted me, beyond all measure, from any other endeavor—the next festival would be dawning on the horizon, in Prague, Warsaw, or Budapest. Sometimes I suspected that these festivals were a conspiracy, conservative forces to block the development of contemporary music. For the secret police could not expect much from us Westerners. Our music may have been played here and there, and given awards, but it was never taken seriously, so we gained knowledge of important events in our own countries exclusively through newspapers. Who had any use for a musician? Every writer, even if he only composed short verses about hazy landscapes in the glare of the sun, was asked to take a position on the state of the world; theater people could flog their political message before a production of the most minor play; journalists and academics got the chance to pontificate again and again; and it even became customary for politicians to be asked to discuss issues of which they were extremely ignorant. But why should one let a musician who wrote nothing but pieces for harp, drums, and Jew's harp comment on important affairs of state? We were not understood, after all. The rules of illusion that we put into practice in our compositions were only accessible to the initiated. The unlimited flexibility of notes was an enigma to most listeners. How did you do that? was the question put to most of us. In the East, of course, it was different; there every musician had access to certain secrets.

As nothing useful could be extracted from musicians, the theoreticians gradually began to be invited, the music philosophers and critics, educated people who could be dragged out of bed at night when one had a craving for a lecture on "Music and Society." They had the patent on ex-

Northbrook Public Library
847-272-6224

02/03/06
01:33 pm

Item:Evidence of love
Due Date: 2/24/2006,23

Mon-Thurs 9-9; Fri 9-6

Sat 9-5, Sun 1-5

www.northbrook.info

plaining our work. And they were easy prey for the secret police, who had to assign their most intelligent people to the project in order not to make themselves look ridiculous. Then a French Communist Party music official, his brow furrowed, could be seen revealing the secret of "musique concrète" to a Polish agent, while at the next table a gifted young editor from a major newspaper in West Germany would be explaining to a man at his table what was actually meant by the slogan "Blow up the opera houses." As more and more nonmusicians were invited to the festivals, the secret police, who, after all, had a limited number of music connoisseurs at their disposal, were no longer able to supervise us, too, so we musicians had ample time for undisturbed exchanges and conversation. Relatively ample. For most of our time was spent listening to welcome speeches, exchanging greetings and toasts to peace and friendship, visiting the houses of local musical luminaries or of musicians of bygone eras, and then sitting through long-winded farewell speeches. In Bratislava, I watched as one of the best-known (and best) German leftist music critics, a professor from Münster or Osnabrück, drank his glass dry at every toast to every delegation; by the end of the opening ceremony, he had to be taken to the hospital in an ambulance. The struggle to save his life took four days, by which time he was fit again for the closing ceremony. On the trip to Munich, I had to hold him over the toilet to vomit every half-hour, because even the slight quantity of alcohol he consumed at the send-off was now enough to turn him into a babbling wreck covered with sweat from head to toe. I have a lot to thank him for though, because, once he

sobered up, he wrote an enthusiastic report on the event in
one of the best German weeklies, in which, while decrying
our age of decadence and musical paralysis on the one
hand and of festivals sprouting like weeds on the other, he
praised the high level of the international participants in
Bratislava and described me as the star of the whole affair.
This in turn helped me receive the largest possible grant for
my own work, personally handed to me by the Bavarian
Minister of Culture. Musicians with a sense of humor
(there are not many, by the way) got what they wanted at
that ceremony, because I was described not only as a virtu-
oso craftsman, but as someone who might one day fulfill
the highest demands of art. May he . . .

So when I received an invitation from Budapest, I was
torn. On the one hand, I was in the middle of my work
and did not want to be distracted under any circumstances;
on the other, I was attracted to the city, which was then
considered a trend-setting place. Beyond that, Munich had
something so self-righteously provincial about it back then
that I finally decided to go. Perhaps I had a kind of premonition not to turn the invitation down, a feeling that something could happen if only I took the first step. Throughout
the summer, I had been able to tame my irritability only
with work; the news from Berlin and Frankfurt made me
angry. The superfluousness of art was now showing its
true face, once the political pressure was gone. Modern art
had become a toy; never would it recover from the politi-
cally motivated attacks on it. And modern music especially,
whose technical cleverness nobody, even those who really
listened to us, could hear, was diminished because it had
no voice in the great council on the definitive formulation

of good taste. Our art was neither decorative nor synthetic. And it was anything but beautiful. A fine art no longer. I hoped things would be different in Budapest. And before long all I thought of anymore was Budapest. Budapest would bring together the last few serious composers; I anticipated Budapest as salvation, the great example, the seed for something new.

So I went to Budapest—by way of Vienna, where I heard a piece of mine performed in such a loveless way that my enthusiasm for Budapest grew in proportion. In order to heighten my excitement, it rained. Yes, it rained all the way from Vienna to Budapest, though the rain was more unpleasant in Budapest than in Vienna; wetter, if one can put it that way; not casual, but insistent, a rain penetrating every nook and cranny. And soon, with the sky nothing but a single hopeless gray block, one no longer knew where the rain came from, above or below. In this apocalyptic scene, I arrived in Budapest; that is, I saw a few houses that the young man who picked me up at the station claimed were part of Budapest. I saw a few cars tunneling through the gray wall of rain, their exhaust fumes dropping to the ground as if producing exhaust were forbidden; even the smoke from the chimneys did not rise into the sky vertically. And occasionally I saw a few hostile-looking people standing at the side of the road, probably waiting for the bus. No matter how hard one tried, it was impossible to imagine they would ever be picked up. But one of the rules of the illusion was to just stand still. Slowly, the will to revolt against these conditions would be paralyzed. At some point, they would all become part of the gray mass, part of the rain.

The young man, Miklos, a student at the conservatory, took me to my lodgings, a kind of barracks said to be in the center of town; all the foreign guests were being housed there. As I got out, I saw what looked like bullet holes in the walls of the buildings. A reception committee had planted itself in the foyer to greet the musicians, all soaked from the short run from the street to the building. I had to hand over my passport and fill out two forms; then I was served one of those inimitable Hungarian schnappses that can bring someone given up for dead back to life. They make one resistant to depression; enjoyed in sufficient quantities, they pull the centrifugally fleeing flesh together and, in next to no time, produce a body that—at least at first glance—is solid. And they taste so good. All the sweetness and bitterness that schnapps distilling has ever invented can be tasted in every drop. I held the glass out again, and without a moment's delay, it was refilled by a sullen old lady. So I was in Budapest; now my life could change.

My room faced the street. Actually, I was supposed to share it with an Italian trombonist, but he had canceled, thank God. There were two beds in the tiny room, and they filled it. For writing, there was a hinged board attached to the wall, which had to be folded if one wanted to reach the bed; but when one sat on the bed, one could write on the board. I felt like Young Törless. Enigmatic Hungary!

In the evening, after the welcome ceremony, there was a lecture by a German literary scholar on "The High Tone in Contemporary German Poetry." Out of solidarity with the speaker, Gert Trares, who taught German literature at the College of Retail Sales in Clausthal-Zellerfeld—I had never read his work or even heard his name before—I walked through the rain to the main lecture hall of the Philosophical Faculty, where the event was to take place. The front rows were reserved for guests of the music festival; the students sat behind us. As I had arrived late, I had to squeeze between two African musicians who had taken over more than a third of my seat and made no effort to accommodate me. Both had put on headphones to listen to an English translation of Professor Trares's remarks, which commenced immediately, as if he had waited for me. He began by listing a few names guilty of the high tone. As nobody in the room knew who the accused were, there was instant commotion, and as Professor Trares had forgotten or misplaced the page on which he had justified his accusations, he read the list of names again. The two Africans then laughed so heartily that, seated between them, I had to hop along with them, which in turn had a contagious effect on the front rows, where people began to giggle, until a nest of laughter was created, an island of merriment that greeted every new name. Only when the lecturer quoted the poems of the representatives of the high tone was there a moment of silence, which I used to regain my seat, inch by inch. The rows were emptying: first the French left the hall, shaking their heads, and gradually the rest of Western Europe followed. The jet-lagged Asians removed their headphones and nodded off. The man to my right had also had it, and put his heavy head on my shoulder with a sigh. I wondered whether the government sent such professors out into the world in order to save money; indeed, one could hardly imagine that a single listener here would afterward feel any desire to visit a Goethe Institute to learn the German language. However, I could not pursue this idea further because now Professor Trares announced that he would begin the second part of his reflections and name those who had *not* been guilty of the high tone. That was too much even for the well-meaning listeners who could speak German and who, until then, had held out. They left the room, some in protest, because by then even Paul Celan and Ingeborg Bachmann had been banished from German literary history. Admittedly, Professor Trares was in top form when he presented the poet Klaus Kottwitz as a shining counterexample. Unhappily, this poet had drunk himself to death a few years earlier, so he was never able to complete the promising work he had begun, and equally unfortunately, his poems, twelve of which, at least, could be attributed to him beyond all doubt, had never been collected for publication. But, Professor Trares announced with noticeable satisfaction, even the closest examination could not reveal a single high tone in these texts. The late Goethe, Heine, and then Kottwitz—that is about how the remaining members of the audience in the Budapest lecture hall were told to imagine the development of modern poetry in Germany. When Trares then prepared to read one of Kottwitz's twelve confirmed poems from a ragged literary journal, the last of the audience left, and with them my African neighbor, who certainly could not be said to have lacked staying power. Kottwitz, Kottwitz, he shouted into the room, shaking his mighty head, and vanished out the door as loud laughter from outside splashed into the lecture hall. I was ashamed, and squirmed in my chair as anger and disgust rose in me, but I stayed until the end, until Professor Trares looked up, took off his glasses, and asked: And what's left? Kottwitz is left, I heard a woman's voice call, a dark, clear alto voice that, as I now saw, belonged to a young woman who was also preparing to leave the hall of horror, with the last of the Hungarian contingent. In the front row, there were still two young composers from East Germany who wanted to discuss the high tone with the professor, while from the back the caretaker approached, who also wanted to put an end to this charade. So I too slipped out.

I made my way through the crowd in the foyer, where everybody was splitting their sides laughing at Professor Trares and his theory of a conspiracy of the high tone that had infiltrated West German society in the guise of poems. Whenever two of them raised their glasses in a toast, they cried: Kottwitz, Kottwitz! So at least the name of the poet who had died of alcoholism was left.

As I had no desire to apologize for my countryman's pathetic nonsense, I lowered my head and walked through the cheerful crowd into the open. Although the rain had let up, it was still wet and clammy. In front of the building, three buses with feebly lit windows were waiting to take the participants back to the barracks, but I wanted to find the way myself with the help of a little map I had found in our welcome to Budapest kit. Unable to decide whether to turn right or left, I rotated the city map in my hands. Then the woman who had called out behind me in the lecture hall strode up beside me. Come with me, I've got an umbrella, she said, putting her arm in mine and pulling me down the flight of steps to the street. We didn't talk much.

Babits lived here, she said; Bartók was often in this house; up there, where the light is shining, is where Lukács lives. As we crossed and recrossed the Danube, I had the impression we were walking in circles. In the middle of still another bridge, she suddenly stopped, looked at me, and said: We should go to a bar now, or else to bed; I have to save my voice for tomorrow, for the high notes. Of course, I absolutely wanted to go into a bar, because the idea of the barracks seemed unbearable. So we went to a wine bar in a godforsaken neighborhood, a kind of artists' club, where she drank tea and I drank a beer and a schnapps and we gazed at each other. Don't look at me so closely, she said, the lecture has aged me. But I never stopped looking at her face, as if I had to memorize it forever. My name is Maria Zuhaczs and tomorrow evening I'll be singing your Mandelstam songs, she said suddenly. Oh, was all I could muster, and even that minimalist statement sounded embarrassing and inappropriate. Late that night, after she had told me her whole life story and I had told her half of mine, she took me to the barracks in a taxi. See you tomorrow, she said. See you tomorrow, I answered.

In the gloomy lobby, a few stalwarts were sitting together over a bottle of wine, among them my African neighbor from the lecture hall, who waved to me with both hands and cried Kottwitz, Kottwitz! Kottwitz, I called back, and ran up the steps as if I were running for my life.

Maria and I were together for four days. As she lived at home with her large family, we had to go our separate ways every night at daybreak. On two evenings, she performed with the opera, in supporting roles; on the evening after we met, she sang my songs. I sat in the last row and fought back tears, because I thought my settings for the Mandelstam poems (in Celan's translation) had never sounded so beautiful. Afterward, the director invited me up on stage for the applause, which gave me the chance to take Maria in my arms in front of everyone and kiss her. A moving moment, I was later told by my African friend, who had come to the concert dressed in his country's splendid national costume, very moving indeed.

For the weekend ahead, Maria had found an apartment where we could celebrate our triumph in peace—our evening of songs had already been declared the high point of the festival. The apartment belonged to a poet she knew well, a recipient of the National Prize. A kind of Hungarian Kottwitz, she said, but with a huge body of work. I received several keys and an exact description of how I could open the various doors to the inner shrine. The street where Pal Friedrich's apartment was—that was the Pannonian panegyrist's name—was perpendicular to the Danube. If we lean far enough out the window, we'll be able to see Lukács's bedroom, she said; but my plans did not include leaning out the window. I wanted to get married.

13

Back then, in order to see each other in peace, we often arranged to meet at the National Museum, where we could talk in front of the paintings in the weakly lit rooms. The long arm of museum pedagogy had not yet reached Budapest; the paintings slept a deep sleep barely disturbed by visitors. As only a few galleries had been restored, one could pass close to the treasures without being reprimanded by the guards, retirees who were as drowsy as the paintings they were sitting on low stools to protect. Thefts of art were unheard of then. Without causing much of a stir, one could confidently have taken down several of the smaller works and subjected them to minute inspection in the light from the windows. Right before the lunch break, and then again before closing time in the evening, there was some movement in the oddly ossified rooms: the guards stood up and stretched; then, sighing and shuffling, they checked whether there were any eccentrics holding out in front of the sumptuously laid tables of the still lifes, in front of the hams and grapes, the pheasants and partridges, the cheeses and other delicacies that—at least in such abundance—could not be found anywhere else in the city. The splendid gloom of the environment, where art could prove the power of illusion, was the perfect setting for our whispered exchanges.

Let's go see the paintings, Maria would say to me softly in the hall at the conservatory, while Romanian horn players and Bulgarian pianists stood around us like a wall, cloaked in a misfortune that could be broken neither by courage nor by hate, but only by perfection. Every one of those overgrown children had no thought other than winning a prize, which would enable them to play in Warsaw, too, and later in New York, where they would live in an apartment on Park Avenue, with recording contracts for wallpaper. And we Westerners were to be the eye of the needle through which they could reach that promised land, we of all people, who had come to Budapest to reconcile music and society. Yet we could do nothing for our red-eyed colleagues in badly fitted suits and rustling taffeta dresses but tell them why the "disappearance of the mortar between the notes" was a necessary development.

There was always someone standing around and listening, of course, the ear that gathered and arranged the dejection (which somehow always culminated in the victory of scores) and probably passed it on to a higher ear that, in turn, was in communication with a bony hand responsible for stamping passports. Let's go see the paintings, Maria whispered to me, so I passed off a stupid lie, left the building, and made my way circuitously to the museum.

It was a hot day. People walked close to buildings still scarred by the bullet holes of war and rebellion, or stole past the trees from shadow to shadow. Thick clusters had formed at the street stands—sweaty children with sluggish mothers, and soldiers, hats under their arms as they eyed the women.

To get to the museum, one had to change trams twice, so I always walked. In one of the few lively streets, which I took as a short cut, I saw ahead of me, within shouting distance, an old man leaning against a tree, sliding to the ground with a scraping sound. I quickly ran up to him and offered assistance—he was breathing heavily and clearly in no condition to get up from the dust by himself. Where do you live? I asked as I draped his arm over my shoulder, and let this wild-eyed man, who incidentally spoke excellent German, lead me to the front door of a building, which, taking the key from his jacket, I unlocked. Just as we stepped into the cool hallway, I saw Maria out of the corner of my eye, standing a short distance away in the street, but I was not able to wave or call to her, because the old man pushed ahead, stumbling, and the door shut behind us with a bang. He lived on the third floor; the elevator was not in service. Hasn't been for a long time, he said, so I carried him up the steps, which wasn't much of a problem, as he was very thin. It was more of a trick to unlock the apartment door, but after I made several attempts the complicated security system finally surrendered.

Then everything was simple. After I laid the man down on his sofa, fetched his medicine from the bedroom, and made tea, new life stole into his old bones, and after I made it clear that he could let himself be spoiled by a stranger with no bad conscience or protest, he began to tell me his life story. He had known everybody, but had never become

well-known himself. Thank God, he said. Otherwise, I'd
no longer be alive. A kind of cowardice had kept him from
speaking out, even though he had been a member of the
party from an early age, first in Vienna, then in Berlin. He
had fought in the Spanish Civil War with Arthur Koestler,
whom he had seen again recently, and he asked that I get a
book from his desk, which was dedicated to "Dear Andras
in memory of the Spanish Civil War." He didn't think
much of Lukács (a nasty character, unfortunately, and a
cruel traitor); he talked about the show trials and about
Belá Balasz (with whom he had written a screenplay in
1925, which had been bought but sadly never filmed), and
about Egon Erwin Kisch and Hanns Eisler, whose raw,
cheerful voice he tried to imitate. The effort made him
cough so hard that, as his temporary physician, I had to
prescribe a break in the flow of his narrative. He had
clearly not spoken for a long time. And clearly this rail-thin
little man had chosen me as someone he could talk to
about his life, and someone to warn not to pile up too
many unfinished projects. Everything he had done was po-
litically motivated—nothing was ever completed. A life
made up of nothing but plans: from the socialist ideas of
his youth to his failed literary career; from hopes of getting a foothold in the movies in America to a job with
Hungarian radio that lasted only three months. Too many
lives are used up so one can succeed, he insisted; here, it's a
hundred to one.

I sat in my chair and listened. I opened the window to
let some air into the stuffy room. Though the sky was over-
cast, there were no signs of an impending thunderstorm

that would rid the air of humidity. While old Andras kept on talking about the darkening of the world, the skies began to clear, and when I was finally able to serve him some soup and had treated myself to a bottle of wine, the heated description of his life was cooled by a gust of fresh evening air.

I've been among rogues my entire life; I've fallen and been dishonored, he said. Now nothing's left for me but killing time rereading old books. The most ridiculous, shiftless, heartless, and selfish people are in power, a slovenly gang that's put history on the wrong track.

When his voice turned into a hoarse rattle, I began to get ready to go. Then I remembered Maria, who had been waiting for me for hours in front of the museum.

I have to go; someone's waiting for me, I said. After I had helped him to his feet so he could close the door behind me and secure it against burglars, I asked one last question: What did he think of Maria's family?

The man sat down again. Watch out, he said, trembling; that whole family's in cahoots with the secret police. If you want to bring misfortune on yourself, get involved with them.

That cryptic sentence pursued me as I ran through the cooling streets of Budapest. It was in my head when I got to the hostel, and it did not subside when, without opening the letter from Maria that the porter gave me, I finally went to bed and tried to get some sleep.

14

Pal Friedrich's apartment building was supposed to be located on a street perpendicular to the Danube, I was told, near the building where Lukács lived. But the street was nowhere to be found. I had gone back and forth through a labyrinth of streets three times and every time ended up at the Danube, cloaked in my raincoat and enveloped in not entirely encouraging thoughts about the future, which I vainly tried to shake off and drown. The harder it became to find the street, the more ridiculous the whole adventure seemed, though that morning I had still thought of it as a lifesaver, and secretly hoped, against all reason, that it would afford me a different angle on myself. My protagonism and antagonism, the double bind that threatened to tear me to shreds, was supposed to be clarified by a fresh perspective. Others went to India to discover the narrow corner of their soul; I had gone to Budapest and met a musician whose soothing or exciting qualities would, I hoped, transcend my inner limitations. But now, leaning on a cold wall and staring at the

dark water as it softly gurgled past, the opposite had come
to pass: in a sense, I had arrived at my old self once again,
depressingly analyzing the consequences of the adventure
I had anticipated, until it had disintegrated into a hundred
details that seemed so very mistaken, pathetic, and im-
moral that I would have liked to run back to my hostel to
continue the dreary discussion of the social conditions of
music, a discussion that was surely getting nowhere without me.

But I wanted to give it one more try. It was now
shortly after ten; Maria would arrive in an hour if the applause stayed within reason, by which time I was to have
heated up the apartment and cooked a meal to create the
best conditions for what I now felt to be burdensome, un-
reasonable, and morally lax. The thought of what went
into getting hold of the apartment for the weekend was
embarrassing, and the memory of the words I had uttered
to Maria to convince her to spend the weekend with me
was growing even more embarrassing. I had gone so far in
my promises and protestations that even I could assume
she would see through my behavior as clowning, as an entertaining performance by a Westerner who knew all too
well that he would be leaving the country in a week, but
clearly my desire to be seen through was disguised by a
much more effective masquerade. I now thought I would
have preferred it if Maria had been able to convince me to
apply for a new visa for the spring, so that after time had
passed, after I had made a careful examination, I could appear before her with determination, with a well-developed
plan; instead, she had immediately done everything she

could to find an apartment for the final weekend of my stay in Budapest: this love nest, as she put it—to my horror, as if I had not done everything I could to make my excessively effusive courting seem like consciously vain courting, as a clear warning not to get involved with me. But as has so often been the case in my life, my clowning, which was supposed to be transparent, was taken as an invitation to devote attention to the real person who concealed himself behind the mask, with a serious person and serious musician, a vulnerable artist who needed disguise in order not to be destroyed by a banal society utterly oblivious to modern music. But I knew only too well that I never would have got Maria's attention without exaggeration and provocation, without verbal fits, which were in essence ambushes, and that without the masquerade she never would have seen me as someone she wanted to have a so-called adventure with. I had already begun to despise her a little for her inability to distinguish the insincere from the sincere, for having fallen for the mask; but even as I thought I should despise her, I despised myself for thinking she was banal. After all, she's infinitely more clever than I am, I thought, staring into the delicate eddies and ripples of the Danube, so she'll have foreseen the embarrassment that would descend on me in anticipation of this weekend and she'll do everything she can to not let such embarrassment ruin the weekend.

While I was trying to find some justification for setting out for a fourth time to find my way to the apartment, a dog joined me, a mangy specimen with strangely protruding ears that looked as if they had been screwed onto the sides of his head; he clearly wanted to share my fate. He had one eye on the bag, out of whose mesh poked brown wrapping paper containing fish and vegetables, as well as the sausage I had bought for breakfast; his other eye, though, or so I imagined, had understood my problem; its dark friendliness was only for me, the ascetic melancholic. Because we were standing opposite Lukács's house, I dubbed him György, which he seemed to like, for he immediately wiggled his misshapen ears in a friendly way. I fed him little pieces of sausage, which, sitting on his hind legs, he swallowed eagerly, without chewing; and he told me his hair-raising story, which, despite the exaggerations all Hungarian dogs are prone to when it comes to sausage, I liked so much that I had no choice but to throw the tail end into his jaws. György, I said, after he had claimed he knew every cobblestone in this grand neighborhood, if you're as clever as you claim to be, then show me the building where the writer and good Communist Pal Friedrich's apartment is. György got up, stretched, opened his muzzle wide, and set off, past the sleeping houses that were now as familiar to me as if I had grown up on the dark streets. He turned left and then left again, until we actually arrived at the street I was looking for, and stopped in front of number 16, where lived the famous poet Pal Friedrich, who was spending the weekend at a writers' congress in Moscow and who, as one of his country's outstanding artists, was faithfully transforming the suffering that accompanied the creative process into radiant verses, to the joy of the working classes. Maria had given me a volume of his essays, published in the GDR, with a hand-written dedication that covered the entire endpaper and concluded with an awk-

ward heart he had drawn beside his name. I had paged
through this book the evening before, but was so distracted by the heart I could not grasp the deeper importance of his work. In the morning, the book lay beside my
pillow as if I had never read it, its green cover warning me
against trying to read it again.

Thank you, György, I said to the dog and opened the
gate according to the instructions I had received from
Maria, who seemed to know her way around here; then I
closed it behind the two of us and made my way up the
steps like an intruder to the third landing; there, in the dim
light of a single bulb, I found apartment No. 32, where
I was supposed to experience our adventurous weekend,
which had been taking on an increasingly frightening shape
in my imagination.

The building was breathing; one could hear it. I bent
over the banister and, with my head at an angle, listened
into the darkness of the shaft as if to make sure nobody
had followed me. Occasionally, a laugh fluttered through
the stairwell; then I heard music, as well as a loud, desperate voice calling someone's name. I was at my wit's end. I
put the key into the lock of the apartment door and turned
it slowly. I felt like a cheap scoundrel, and a common bur-
glar to boot, who, having been smuggled in from the West,
intended to penetrate the heart of Eastern artistry. But a
third feeling was there, too, of which I had only a shadowy
sense: one of walking into a trap. The stupidity with
which I was performing this break-in was so evident that if
charges were filed, I might be able to plead mitigating
circumstances. More likely, the death sentence would immediately be carried out. In any case, I was out of place,

followed by a dog with mangy fur; I did not belong here. My heart was beating painfully loudly, my blood rushing to my head, my entire body overcome by a trembling that was tearing my skin from my bones. Even the disciplined György had been infected by this uncomfortable state of mind, for he suddenly lay down like a rolled-up carpet, panting, pressing himself against the door, and sniffing at the crack as if a paradise of meat were behind it. Suddenly I felt an urge to laugh. For a second, I saw myself through the eyes of the secret police: a Berlin composer bending down in front of a stranger's keyhole, close to fainting, his body shaking and sweating, accompanied by a whimper-ing Hungarian dog. I had to do something.

As I cautiously began to open the now unlocked door, a wave of stench overwhelmed me, a stench so unpleas-antly acrid that both of us, György and I, stumbled away from the door in panic; in my uncontrolled attempt to flee I stepped on the dog's paw, and he responded with a cry of pain that exceeded all imaginable expressions of pain.

A bearded man with horn-rimmed glasses that uncan-nily magnified his already wide-open eyes stepped out onto the landing from apartment 31 next door, to find him-self confronted by a stranger crouching on one knee be-side a whimpering dog and trying to comfort it with German endearments. Whether he had been hardened by similar experiences or whether he was accustomed to such performances from his prominent neighbor, the noisy confusion did not seem to unsettle him. What can I do for you? he asked in an anachronistically familiar Ger-man, and at first all I could do to answer was point at Pal

Friedrich's open apartment, from which the acrid smell, the true cause of our miserable condition, was streaming as powerfully as ever.

The bearded man, who later turned out to be an outcast university lecturer devoted to hermeneutics (which had clearly deadened his sense of smell), walked into the apartment with the mincing steps of the short-sighted, felt around for the light switch, and invited me and the dog in. The moderately lit hall was lined with shelves full of randomly stacked books. Piles of photographs, rocks, feathers, and assorted other junk gathered dust on the floor. While the lecturer waited at the door, the dog and I forged deeper into this tunnel of books, like two explorers, I fanning myself first with my hands and later with a State Prize certificate. Then even the dog held back, cowering on a bast carpet, his head on his paws, whimpering with fear. At the end of the hall, I turned around and, as if through a telescope, saw the dog stretched out flat on the floor and the bearded philosopher in the apartment door, making odd hand movements. I opened the living room windows and let in the cold, damp air. Then I sat down in a leather armchair by the open window and took ten deep breaths, counting them on my fingers. Perhaps I have no talent for adventure, I suddenly thought, just as I have no talent for being happy or for total devotion, and perhaps all of my adventures—or anything I wanted to remember as an adventure—were only guided undertakings meant to drive me into a state of confusion, to make me lose my bearings. So was Maria my guide? Had she lured me into a writer-functionary's stinking apartment to test my character?

I got up and turned on every available light source to illuminate this shadowy realm, but not even that measure could drive the foul stench out of the room. It had over-whelmed every object with ruthless peculiarity; it lay like a layer of dust on the coffee table, the chairs, the pictures, and the books. With a gloomy expression György made his way over to me, then dragged himself limping to a door plastered with faded, brownish posters, which he scratched energetically with his uninjured paw. I followed him and opened this door, too, though I should have known by then that every door in this kingdom of death would open on a terrible display. The pale beam of light fell on a bed covered with dark cloths, on which sat three anxiously squealing, utterly exhausted cats with glazed eyes, looking as if they had been prevented from vanishing into feline heaven against their will. I had never before wit-nessed greater misery, not in Budapest and not anywhere else. In response to my tentative calls, the animals tried to rise from the piles of excrement, but they fell back down, collapsing into a frayed little heap. Even György was stunned into inaction by the sight; a picture of outrage. And on this bed, I suddenly thought, on this bed drenched in cat piss, Maria wanted us to celebrate an early wedding.

Where was Maria anyway?

To get to the kitchen, I had to go back through the hall, where the lecturer was still waiting at the bright end, as if eavesdropping. Come, please help, I called to him; something bad has happened here, but he seemed to think my request was a trick. What happened? he asked.

I had to go past the dusty classics of Socialist Realism all the way to the door and pull the reluctant man into the enemy's realm by force, for, as he later confessed, he had taken it to be a perfidious scene staged by the secret police, who could easily have gone into the apartment in his absence to rummage through his hermeneutic writings, which—unprotected and easily accessible, as he put it— filled his room. But he turned out to be a willing, if not very helpful, assistant, and we set about bringing the neglected cats back to life. We cleaned the animals and fed them my fish, my love banquet, and bedded them down beside the radiator in an emptied desk drawer of the socialist master of the sonnet, from which, wrapped in towels, they gazed curiously at the ambitious operations we undertook to reinstate order. The bed linen, along with all the bedspreads, was pulled off and thrown onto the balcony, which was covered by cases of empty bottles; as we were working well together, a few other things followed the bed linen, and finally we threw the mattress on top of it all to air out in the wintry Budapest night. Mr. Bela, as the hermeneutician asked me to call him, quite enjoyed this forbidden activity, so I had no problem convincing him to banish what did not suit us into the bedroom, until only the armchairs were left in the living room, along with the coffee table and a desk, so that the feeling now was minimalist, yet reasonably homey. That done, we took first one and later two more bottles of Tokay from the kitchen cupboard and made ourselves comfortable in the armchairs, wrapped in our coats. I fed György a can of Bulgarian sardines, Mr. Bela fetched his pipe, and I supplied myself with a Cuban cigar I found in a box on the bookshelf. Who would have expected the evening to turn out so entertaining?

Bela began the uninterrupted account of his research with the deeply shocking and often uproarious details of his expulsion from the university, which had basically meant the exclusion of the hermeneutic method from Hungarian philosophy. He described himself as an extra in a miserable story that was part of the miserable trends in postwar Hungarian thought; he had even had to provide the terminology that the professors used to attack him. But as he recalled every humiliation he had suffered, he himself gradually became the core of the argument, and I gained the decided impression that without him there would be no Hungarian philosophy at all. His stubborn resistance had guaranteed its survival, but his refusal to follow the official line had also strengthened the hand of his adversaries. It crossed my mind that if I were to secure a position in West Germany for him, the entire system of philosophical education in Hungary would inevitably collapse. In short, precisely because Mr. Bela could no longer hope to become the leading exponent of progress, he kept the hope of a Marxist Hungarian philosophy alive. As for him, he no longer believed that anything like a Marxist philosophy was possible, and the idea of a liberal-Marxist aesthetic, which I outlined in a few words, made him laugh so hard that the half-starved cats and the dog raised their heads in astonishment. His rhetorical technique consisted of asking questions that he promptly answered himself, as if he had practiced this game in the many hours of his solitude. Can any reasonable human being imagine a Marxist aesthetic? he asked in my direction, and immediately followed the question with a resounding *no* that made his mighty beard tremble. Those no longer capable of desiring the impossible can only create what is all too possible, he shouted. Please look at our art, our art produced according to the dictates of Marxism, and you'll find only the half-finished and the sluggish, or else the stupefied and the cumbersome, an ominous bustle of activity stripped of the power of the soul, and although we thought that Communist revolution would create something wholly new and awesome, everything on display in the state galleries is misshapen and on the lowest possible level, without any sign of the promised transformation. An impure, closed, impenetrable situation. The life of the spirit can't be maintained simply by continuing the bad and the mediocre, by a relative, gradual depreciation of the means of artistic work and of thought.

After we'd blocked the ways back into the past, what was left for us to do but head into the open? But the open frightened us and provided a reentry for the worst elements of the past, terrible artistic fads. We're sitting here in the armchairs of one of those terrible artists and drinking the wine of this terrible artist, whose art consists of filling the great sonnet form with a tiny socialist content.

Had I not come to Hungary to reflect upon Marxist aesthetics with my colleagues? And now there I was, sitting and listening with growing equanimity to the beautiful humming of age-old European erudition, a conceptual tightrope walk over nothingness between two irreconcilable cliffs.

The alcohol helped me follow this harangue, and the more I drank, the easier it became to penetrate Mr. Bela's inner workshop, where his unfolding ideas ran riot into myths. Whenever he paused in his long, complex sentences, he looked as if he were about to make a request, and his eyes begged me to guess what that request might be. But I only sat in my leather armchair and nodded from time to time, until he had caught his breath again. I didn't know what powers had called on him to raise his voice in such an overblown way, but I was not surprised when, after long, complicated sequences of words, he began to talk about God, for whom one had to have unqualified devotion, so as not to deprive us of his concern. That's all we can do, he insisted, chewing dreamily on his beard. We have to call our own word into general history, not the Party's word. We have to accept the past as the prehistory of our lives, in order to understand the development of art as the expression of our existence. Our existence does not date to the October Revolution, my dear sir, as the professors who hounded me from the university believe. A mob of half-educated criminals who've bound the highest to the lowest, the sublime to the shameful. How is one supposed to win the future that way, he asked, poking in his pipe.

I couldn't answer. Flabbergasted, I sat in my sticky leather armchair and tried to look halfway intrigued. The concept of a "nurturing unity," which he had evoked several times to connect Plato and Kant, buzzed through my head and left a trail that I tried to provide a melody for. What was my own "nourishing unity"? Music, fine. But, if I were to believe my new philosophical friend, wasn't I on the verge of betraying that ultimate source to an ideology?

Only Christianity, Bela interrupted my reflections, only Christianity is in a position to draw the mystery out of nothingness and plant it in the individual; only Christianity knows those metaphors for the nameless one that distinguish the great religious teachings. No art, and above all no Marxist art, will ever be in a position to make up for the lack created by the foolish erasure of Christianity. No art, no matter how avant-garde, can replace the elementary power of the great teachings. By the way, all the great teachings come from the East, Bela said with a laugh, but from farther east than the Warsaw Pact states. Nothing comes from us at all. We have nothing more to offer. Our store is empty. The only people who still visit us are Western intellectuals in search of truth. Good God, how foolish they are. And it won't take much longer for the East to come visit you, my dear sir, and if you have nothing more to offer than a few museums and churches turned into museums, a few Marxist philosophers and a few coins, then God have mercy on you.

At a certain point, the flow of his words, which after all his years of solitude had finally found a listener, must have sent me to sleep. In any case, I suddenly startled out of a ghastly nightmare and banged my feet against the coffee table with such force that the three bottles that had formed a peaceful still life tipped over and rolled off the edge one after another, where they landed on the dog, who had exchanged Bela's tirades about the empty West for a deep sleep a while ago. He looked at me so sadly, with his oddly positioned ears, that I slid out of my chair onto the floor and began to pet him. Only then did I notice that the other armchair was empty. The hermeneutician had apparently returned to his apartment to continue work on his theory of "turning back," because, as he imagined it, only that could fill what God had made of the world with life. But as I pondered those words, the last I was conscious of having taken in, I suddenly heard a shrill laugh. It was Maria. And just as I was about to take the dog and go look for the laughing woman, she suddenly came through the door with the philosopher. The lecture would go on, then, I thought. And if Maria had not thrown herself on me with a loud cry and covered my entire face with kisses, the hermeneutician, who had placed the fourth and fifth un-corked bottles in front of himself, would have continued with his damnation of the dismal temporal world, which he wanted to clearly distinguish from the eternal world of tradition. By then, I had succumbed to Bela's words so unreservedly that Maria's incessant kissing—which was supposed to make me forget her unforgivably late arrival—seemed inappropriate, if not embarrassing. So, whenever she pummeled my neck with her wet lips, I made signs over her head to the philosopher to continue with his dis-course. But there was no salvation. It was a while before Maria finally released me—too long a while, in any case, to allow me to give philosophy its due. Still, even Bela seemed pleased by his short-term release from serious thought, for he sat there with his legs stretched out, relax-ing in the absent and despised Communist poet's armchair while he drank the poet's heavy Tokay, while Maria lis-tened until the end of the fifth bottle to my report about why we had waited for her with the windows open, cloaked in our coats. György and the cats listened, too.

It was 3:14 A.M. when, suddenly, Bela collapsed with a whimper. Maria knew it was hopeless to try to bring him back to consciousness, so she helped me out of my chair, fished the apartment key out of Bela's jacket, and, after closing the windows and turning off the lights, guided me to the adjacent apartment, where we settled into Bela's unmade bed as if it were the most natural thing in the world.

15

Within a few weeks of my departure from Budapest, I received news from Maria for the first time—in Munich, where I had gone in search of the better living conditions. The atmosphere in Berlin had not been conducive to making music. Too much revolution, too few string quartets. As the postal service was essentially an appendage of the secret police, Maria and I had agreed not to entrust the proofs of our love to the mail. And because we had no intention of denying our intimate relationship, private individuals were called upon to perform that task. Even they were not to be burdened with any unambiguous correspondence, however, so our messages had to be transmitted via poems or newspaper clippings. As a result I often found myself brooding over badly translated texts by Pétöfi or Ady. Despite conscientious exegesis, I never could grasp how the pain they described was applicable to us. A volume of Ady's poems, in which Maria had pasted dried flowers between particular pages, was particularly hard to understand. In the end, I could recite the poems in question by heart, but without recognizing the lines that were meant to hold our relationship together. So nothing was left for me but to interpret the world-weariness Ady exuded, in a rendition by a brave East German translator, as the basis of our divided existence. In those days we took anything and everything, from the most trifling matters to international political events, as signs intended exclusively for us anyway, and so even Endre Ady's innocent, pathetic poems were colored by our secret exchange.

One beautiful and unusually hot spring day, I received a call from a music critic who wanted to meet me in private to deliver news from Budapest. This man's reputation was extraordinary. He had published only a few short essays in out-of-the-way journals, essays written so tersely that only hardened supporters read them all the way through, but the effect of his minimalist production was astonishing. Wherever he happened to be, he was met with a mixture of fear and respect. His message was complex in its expression, but easy to reproduce: the history of music was over, all musical material exhausted. The scorn with which he blasted anything still definable as formal composition made even the most sophisticated work wilt. Not even I could hope to find favor with him, and during our phone call I gloomily surveyed page one of my second string quartet, spread in front of me on my desk.

He suggested we meet in a beer garden that he had learned to appreciate on earlier visits to the city for the quality of its wine. I personally avoided beer gardens and would never have thought one might serve especially good wine. I immediately suspected he wanted to confuse me. When I hung up, I found it impossible to continue working. After his many hints and insinuations I first had to put my thoughts in order. He had been in Krakow at the New Music Festival, nothing worth mentioning, he said, but still interesting. One of the last great European cabalists lives in Krakow: Professor Peterkiewicz, with whom he had had the pleasure of speaking. After meeting Peterkiewicz, he canceled his scheduled lecture on capitalism and music, subjects whose meaninglessness was all too obvious, and instead had gone onstage with Peterkiewicz to discuss the concept of *teschuba* (turning back), which, he thought, was of enormous importance for the dubious future of music. I assume you know what area opens up behind the concept of *teschuba*, he had asked on the phone, and because all I produced was a vague sound, he said he was ready, later in the beer garden, to provide a brief summary of the ideas he had worked out with Peterkiewicz in Krakow. Maria had also attended the gathering and enthusiastically approved; she had given a concert the evening before—a miserably ephemeral event—and had then gone with him and a few other invited guests to Peterkiewicz's house, where they all sat in his library, the best private cabalistic library in Europe, and listened to the revered professor until daybreak. On the way from Peterkiewicz's apartment to their respective accommodations, Maria had entrusted a few words to him that he would communicate to me in person as accurately as possible.

I set out for the beer garden three hours before the appointed time. Some people are exhausting on the phone, even when they are well-meaning and saying something one is eager to hear. Still, listening to them can be a tor-ment. With the celebrated music critic, it was his odd mix-ture of music and cabala that made me sweat as I was listening on the phone, and if he had not been the bearer of Maria's news, I would have hung up.

The street was deserted. Frau Köhler, the caretaker of the apartment, was leaning against the building in the sun, smoking. She nodded at me with a guilty look, though it was not clear whether she wanted to apologize for her smoking or for her idleness. The man at the kiosk handed me newspapers and cigarettes. He always sighed, and sometimes an "Ah!" would escape him, as if to apologize for the news he sold. The wordless conversation he carried on with his customers seemed like the sum of all possible conversations—on politics, the economy, culture, sports. Only a wind-blown sigh gave shape and substance to the man cowering in his cave.

Three girls in uniform with berets on their frizzy hair were sitting at the bar in the café. Probably students from the College of Fashion Design, who had contributed to a visible improvement in the level of fashion in our neigh-borhood. The girls were drinking cola with straws and laughing so hard at the same time that their drinks went up their noses, producing a coughing attack that made them get off their barstools and almost throw up. They had barely managed to catch their breath before another fit of laughter shook them, until they finally staggered out of the café to continue their St. Vitus's dance outside, leaning on a lime tree enveloped in a green shimmer. I had finished drinking my coffee when one of them came back to pay for the three colas. She stood at the counter in high boots, her legs apart, and answered the waitress's question about what had been going on: That's what's so weird; we don't really know. I could see the waitress was disappointed. She would have liked to laugh along with them, even if there was nothing to laugh about. She then sent a searching look across the kitchen counter at me, the only guest at this hour of the day, but I was reading the business section of *Die Zeit*, and there was no grin on my face.

I arrived at the little beer garden a half-hour ahead of time. The sun had gone down, so the customers had gone inside. The headwaiter was there, carefully wiping the tables with a frayed cloth, and two men who were hectically waving their arms. They were the feared music critic, Horst Leisegang, who never wrote, and the equally feared conductor Günter Sofsky, who never conducted, and whose table I now joined with some excitement. Both cultivated an old-fashioned politeness that made conversing with them easy, as it disguised the malicious remarks they made. It was clear that the two had only recently become a couple—always of one mind, finishing each other's sentences. Both had been sitting in the beer garden since the phone call and had drunk several bottles of a light wine from Baden, which considerably improved the conversation. Before long we had laid the foundation for our discourse: none of the orchestras in Munich was worth a damn, no director was able to get a single acceptable sound out of such rotten performers, the music school should be closed and the faculty sent into factories, the local critics should immediately look for new jobs, and the public should be forbidden to attend concerts. With exquisite politeness, it was communicated to me that I would be better off putting my work on ice for a while, as the situation could not be expected to improve in the near future. Everyone involved in the music industry would be well advised to keep their eyes open for other job opportunities. Perhaps we should all become teachers, and teach the spoiled pupils to read music, but under no circumstances encourage them to do any creative work. Art must disappear, the conductor gleefully shouted, thus finding a simpler form for what the critic had previously proposed in carefully chosen words. Art had alienated people from society; ever since just about everybody had become an artist, and the state had capitulated to them and set up more institutes and institutions to train the masses of would-be artists, anyone could call himself an artist after eight semesters, without knowing anything about art. As a result, German avant-garde music was often played for foreign guests by German musicians, even though everybody knew that neither the composer nor the musicians knew what music worthy of talking about was. The prime minister of Togo, said the conductor, goes back to his African homeland firmly convinced he has heard German music, but in truth he has heard German stupidity, and, as he only rarely has the opportunity to hear it, he'll claim all over the world that what he heard in Munich was German music, which is simply not true. I remember wondering whether the country of Togo still existed and whether the country's prime minister had attended a concert in Munich by

Musica Viva, which seemed highly unlikely, but I kept such thoughts to myself. Togo! What in the world was the prime minister of Togo doing at Musica Viva! If Togo was a country and hence had a prime minister, then the man had come to Munich to ask about foreign aid, not to attend a concert in the Musica Viva series.

The wine had gone to my head. As the evening quickly turned cooler, the words of the two music lovers hardly got through to me anymore. The theoretician's huge head, so reminiscent of Hegel's, fell forward, and his orphic curses were few and far between; the conductor had difficulty handling his glass, so he pushed it from the edge of the table inward to safer ground, so slowly that he seemed to be conducting an important experiment.

I called the waiter, who was standing at a safe distance keeping a firm eye on the peculiar group of customers, and asked for the bill, but instead of laboriously adding up four baskets of bread and ten bottles of wine, the friendly man, who we later learned was from Nis, did his best to give us a number he considered fair. To the theoretician's great surprise, the restaurant did not accept checks, so it was left to me to pay the sum, and as the two had not come to Munich on business, after all, but to pass on a message to me, I paid without grumbling. To my own great surprise, the waiter soon came back not only with the change, a ten-mark bill he carried between his teeth, but with two suitcases and a few other bags, some leather and some plastic, which, after I had renounced the ten in his favor, he kept holding until we had finally stood up and were ready to leave. The theoretician walked out empty-handed; the bags were hung on the conductor's shoulders; the two suitcases, which were apparently loaded with books from Professor Peterkiewicz's library, were relegated to me. By the time the conductor and I had stumbled out to the street, the theoretician was already ensconced in the front seat of a taxi, whose back doors and trunk were wide open. You have to give him your exact address and instructions on how to get there, the theoretician announced to me, because, he said, the driver was not yet familiar with the city—a more and more common phenomenon, he added.

So I directed the Pakistani to Schwabing, where I lived in a three-room apartment on Herzogstrasse. Then the taxi driver not only had to turn the music off, but also close all the windows tight, because both the theoretician and the conductor lived in constant fear of drafts and had found the taxis in Krakow, apparently constructed in East Germany exclusively for lovers of fresh air, a deadly means of transport. Incomprehensible, said the conductor, incomprehensible in a city supposedly in love with music. Why socialism was not capable of building airtight, heated, radio-free cars was a riddle to the theoretician, which he asked the silent Pakistani to solve, who, in turn, having answered the question of what he found of special interest about Germany by saying Bismarck, fell silent.

I paid for the taxi and dragged the suitcases to the third floor. What would happen now? Perhaps we could continue the evening with a light meal, suggested the theoretician, while the conductor asked if he could take a bath.

I made noodles; the theoretician fell fast asleep on the couch in my study; the conductor sat singing in the tub and reading a novel by Nabokov he had taken from my shelf. Overrated, he mumbled as he put on his underwear; overrated, but amusing.

I ate my noodles, read Georg Simmel, and was finally drinking a good wine, my last bottle of Barolo, when the conductor, cloaked in a white bath towel I had stolen from a hotel in Venice, tiptoed into the kitchen and asked whether I had a sleeping mask for the master, as the blinds were stuck. I did not have one. I laid a towel on the twitching Hegel face, but it was brushed away. Finally, we put the mumbling theoretician on a blanket and dragged him into my bedroom, where he spent the night in my bed along with his close friend, who had immediately collapsed beside him, breathing hard from the load he had carried. I let the blinds down, closed the windows, wished them a good night, and went into my study to work for an hour or so on my string quartet.

I found it impossible to concentrate. I dug out one of the theoretician's essays from a pile of cultural journals and tried to find out why this basically friendly man abhorred the idea that music was still relevant in this society. But after three pages, I made myself comfortable on the couch, wearily reached for the light switch, and surrendered to sleep.

The next morning, a Friday, the two planned to take a train to Rome around noon; as for me, I wanted to go shopping, then focus on my composition for two and a half days with no interruptions. I wanted to arrange to be back home around eleven, have coffee with the two of them, hear what news there was from Maria, then bundle the two men into a taxi—and exhale.

I slammed the door loudly enough behind me to wake them up. Mrs. Köhler, who was cleaning the stairs, as she did every Friday, looked up at me angrily, for she knew I would come back and track dirt into the stairwell. The one-armed actor who lived below me and was also going shopping told me he had been offered a role in a detective series: he was to play a one-armed man. As if the part had been written for him, he laughed, while, from upstairs, Mrs. Köhler asked when she should turn on the television. When he was on television, he always invited all the tenants to come watch; only Mrs. Köhler was no longer invited, for she had once made disparaging remarks about his acting skills. Mrs. Köhler's husband had been missing for years, and her son was in prison on several counts of grand theft auto, so she had a lot of time to study the listings and to pronounce judgments that, as far as I could tell, were largely accurate.

I got the newspapers from the trembling man and went to the supermarket, where I bought a chicken, a few lamb cutlets, carrots, beans, and potatoes, along with milk, coffee, and a few little things, until nothing was left in my wallet but a twenty-mark bill, which I exchanged at the Lehmkuhl bookstore for a volume from the Bibliothek Suhrkamp collection. I took the change to the ice-cream parlor next door, owned by a red-haired family from Piedmont, and Emilio brought me the best cappuccino in Munich. My friend Hans Never was at the table by the door, brooding over a highly ambitious screenplay, but as young women were constantly entering the place, he was surely not going to get much done. Opposite me, in the darkest corner, the painter Stamm was sitting and doodling in his notebook with a ballpoint. There were a bunch of students there too, along with the several beautiful women who were always in the area, although one could never tell whether they worked—or ever intended to. Oddly austere creatures with esoteric books or fashion magazines under their arms, they came, saw, and conquered, or strolled off again and were immediately replaced, as if from an inexhaustible source.

I read the newspapers and paged through Ernst Bloch's *Spuren*, which I had just purchased, without registering any of it. The hatred of art shown by those two musicians, who nevertheless idolized and lived for art, had drained me. I sat at my table as if petrified; the cappuccino got cold. An unfamiliar rage arose in me, a murderous rage I could only conquer by walking. So I paid, nodded to the painter and to Hans, and walked up and down Leopoldstrasse with my heavy plastic bags until it was at last eleven o'clock.

It was quiet in the apartment. The two suitcases were still in the hall; the door to the bathroom was ajar. A weak smell of coffee announced that the two, or at least one of them, had left the bedroom. In the kitchen, I put the bags down and put the food in the refrigerator especially carefully. Given the prevailing conditions, I, at least, wanted to be sure to do things with care. When there was nothing more to be accomplished in the kitchen, I went through the hall to my study, loudly clearing my throat, and put the newspapers and Ernst Bloch on the windowsill. Paralyzed, I gazed across the roofs and counted more than twenty chimneys; a thin strand of smoke rose out of one of them into a blue sky dotted with a few cumulus clouds.

The conductor stepped up behind me, still—or again—cloaked in my towel. He looked swollen, wrinkled and surly. The phone had wakened them both, he said, but unfortunately too late for their train to Rome. A man from the main office of the Goethe Institute had wanted to talk to me about a chamber music week in Chicago, a Dr. Arnheim; he was in Munich and would come by around 4 P.M. Would I mind if he and the master informally took part in the discussion? They had been wanting to make suggestions for the improvement of the musical work of the Goethe Institute for years, and this was an opportunity. Anyway, the master was now ready to get up, but would appreciate a little glass of wine to combat his morning-after thirst.

So we sat in the kitchen until four o'clock. The chicken was eaten, the new wine drunk. The conductor had done the master's hair and rubbed him down with hot towels. The master read my Bloch out loud and made comments on it, always about the revolution, which he longed for and despised at the same time. When the jovial Dr. Arnheim arrived, he was delighted to find the famous music theoretician, who in turn immediately stuttered out a roundabout recommendation that a Goethe Institute be founded in Venice, a suggestion that Dr. Arnheim conscientiously entrusted to his notebook. Just before six, the conversation was interrupted briefly, as the conductor and the theoretician wanted to fill out their lottery tickets (which had to be turned in by six o'clock), a procedure they performed with downright scientific, even cabalistic precision. Neither they nor I had any cash, so Dr. Arnheim was asked to help out

with a fifty-mark bill, to be paid back to him with 100 per-
cent interest in the event of any winnings, as the master actually wrote down on a piece of paper, which Dr. Arnheim
folded and entrusted to his wallet as carefully as if it were
an incunabulum. His wallet, by the way, contained an astonishing supply of large bills.

An unyielding melancholy came over me at these
strange transactions. The monstrous sense of entitlement
demonstrated by the two musicians was hard to reconcile
with the petty-bourgeois calculation of the lottery numbers (which they had derived from all kinds of combina-
tions). And the clowning misuse of Dr. Arnheim as the
banker for their ridiculous operations contradicted the fact
that they had asked him in all seriousness not to appoint
them to run the Goethe Institute they wanted to see
in Venice (you surely have qualified professionals for that)
but to act as advisers. They wanted to be advisers. There
was too much management in the world of art, and not
enough advice. Moreover, as they already had a palazzo in
mind for themselves in their future role as advisers, they
suggested—after the lottery tickets had been taken care
of—that the top floor of that very palazzo be made available as an apartment for the Institute, as intellectual im-
pulses could also be nourished by proximity to business
operations. In any case, the top floor was fitted with old
Venetian furniture, so it was suitable for official functions
on special occasions. You cannot imagine, the theoretician
insisted to Dr. Arnheim, how much the standing of the
Federal Republic of Germany has suffered as a result of
the furnishing of its institutes abroad. I instantly thought

of Togo, but now we were on to the embassy in Warsaw, whose ghastly seating was almost entirely responsible for the miserable progress of reconciliation with Poland. They had been forced to listen to the cultural attaché in a bent, bowed posture, if posture was even the right word, given such seating. We'd have lain down on the carpet in protest, my dear Dr. Arnheim, if the carpet had not been such a terrible color, like stale urine, said the conductor, with an expression so wretched that Dr. Arnheim put three exclamation marks after his note: *Check color in room of cultural attaché in Pol. residence.* That will be looked into, he insisted. It'll all be taken care of; you'll hear from me soon; I'll go to Venice personally to take a close look at the palazzo.

Later we went to dinner, paid for by the Goethe Institute, at the Osteria in Schellingstrasse, supposedly Hitler's favorite restaurant, the conductor told us. I normally don't get as many suggestions and proposals in an entire year as I've received from you today, Dr. Arnheim said, to justify the enormous bill. Music, needless to say, had not been talked about; it was mentioned in passing, as an item in the Venetian budget, an item which, if the president of the Goethe Institute and the foreign minister properly authorized the new institute (which Dr. Arnheim no longer doubted after the fifth liter of wine), the two advisers would soon control. The comedy had a final, grotesque act: the already drunk Dr. Arnheim suddenly sprang up and stumbled to the door, through which the Bavarian prime minister had just entered, also drunk—glowing with alcohol—accompanied by a few of his vassals, all of them with heavy double chins and the faces of gangsters. And the wobbly head of the Christian Social Union party actually did approach our table, led by the wildly gesticulating Dr. Arnheim, where the conductor and the theoretician were introduced as the future intellectual advisers of the planned Goethe Institute in Venice, while I was dubbed a professor of composition and one of the Institute's important collaborators. Fantastic, said Dr. Tandler; an honor, said Dr. Riedl. But don't neglect Bavarian culture's independent contribution to German culture, added Dr. Strauss. Then we raised our glasses and drained them in half-erect postures. The gentlemen put their glasses down on our table, then turned to their own, where they could concentrate in peace, though loudly, on their corruption scandals.

The deal's done, I think, mumbled Dr. Arnheim, when, with the help of the restaurant owner, I had found a taxi driver who would not only transport the inebriated official but also, in exchange for a lot of money taken from Dr. Arnheim's wallet, haul him into his apartment. Strauss is our witness—were the last words I heard from him.

16

The musicians stayed until the following Tuesday. I set my alarm for 6 A.M., when I stormed into the bedroom with loud shouts, tore open the window, and pulled the bedclothes off before the two were on their feet, to block their retreat. By shortly before eleven, the theoretician had actually been rubbed down, his hair was styled, and he was fortified with coffee. I began transporting the luggage, while the two reluctantly and grumpily followed. The conductor had asked for my edition of Kafka's diaries as reading matter for the trip; the newly purchased *Spuren* blinked from the theoretician's jacket pocket; both books were to be returned on their next visit. I was to claim the four marks thirty they had won in the lottery and buy another ticket, one with the numbers of their birthdays, which they apparently assumed I knew. When the two had finally left, I bought two rolls and the newspapers and went back to my apartment, which seemed unfamiliar and devastated to me, as if I had never lived or worked there before.

From the open car window, the theoretician pulled my head down and whispered into my ear: I do want to tell you what Maria so earnestly insisted I tell you: She's expecting a child.

17

In terrible agony, I finished my second string quartet, which, with texts by Anna Akhmatova, had its premiere in the Radio Building in Cologne. Maria was invited to recite the texts, but I never expected her to do so. Only when I offered to pay for the trip and the honorarium was a telegram sent to her with the terms of a contract. But she turned it down. She was visibly pregnant and wanted to spare her baby the strain and the audience in Cologne the distraction.

The performance was anything but pleasant. There had been too few rehearsals, and the musicians were irritated because the Akhmatova recitation came from a tape that I had recorded myself. Nobody could claim that the work was the slightest bit distinctive; it blurred, fell apart, and ended in tired applause from the invited audience, who had expected something altogether different. Even the usual discussion following the performance did not improve matters. The radio man, well-meaning as he might have been, who had invited me to participate so he would not be stuck with the same old esoterica, openly admitted that he found my piece old-fashioned, if not reactionary, and the third participant in the discussion, a music critic from Cologne, wanted to talk about the issue of "music and society" instead, although without my participation. A great deal was apparently expected of society, which was otherwise so deeply despised. I still remember how, leaning back in my chair, I vanished into a murk, which was only occasionally penetrated by such concepts as "musical fascism" and "stale musical rhetoric"; the rest was society. As nothing more was said about my quartet, and nobody had ever heard of Anna Akhmatova let alone read anything by her, I made no effort to return from my haze to the dreary scene in the Radio Building, which the endlessly chattering critic would interpret in the newspaper two days later as petit-bourgeois arrogance in the face of the great issues of the age. When the torture was finally over, and people were allowed to talk normally and encouraged to head to a nearby restaurant, I disappeared into the toilet, which I didn't leave until I could be sure nobody was there waiting for me. Probably a stupid precaution, as nobody had any desire to drink a beer with the evening's loser anyway. The sense of who the losers were was particularly strong in such local communities; one could almost smell who didn't belong, and besides, the music clique in Cologne had developed a language and corresponding gestures that automatically stamped anyone who had not mastered both as a loser. So I belonged to a group, seemingly respectable, that could have called itself the Not-Cologne School, and could, in turn, be divided into subordinate groups, whose deepest, lowliest fraction consisted of those who accepted lucrative invitations to Cologne only to fail there because they did not know how to find a common denominator for pure music and impure society. I could not; that was clear. All that was left me was to give it a try outside the Cologne School, which was hard enough, or to accept still another invitation to be humiliated in Cologne, which the radio man was ready to offer. The radio regulations required him to schedule a certain percentage of people not from Cologne, and as he sincerely appreciated my willingness to suffer, he kept inviting me and getting composition commissions for me, perhaps because he was unconsciously convinced that my repeated failures might demonstrate the superiority of the Cologne School.

In any case, in spite of the fact that they were denigrated as sentimental nonsense by that school, I had a steady, ongoing success in Cologne with my short pieces for piano, percussion, and alto, which were based on poems by Osip Mandelstam. Today, now that the Cologne School is no more, these lieder are numbered by critics among the most influential pieces in the contemporary renaissance of the form—but they are never played in Cologne anymore.

I walked through the dense darkness along the Rhine, whose softly singing water would not let me go. In that hour before midnight, I was no longer sure whether I should keep composing. I would receive commissions, fellowships, and prizes in the future, of course, because my name had been prominently mentioned too often to be suddenly forgotten. And why shouldn't I accept a professorship that I had refused in the past in order to first write the main sections of the works I had planned. I was not worried about my livelihood; nor was I anxious about my social status. Even the money from the summer courses I had given in Iowa for years was enough for me to live comfortably.

Maria was with me as I walked along the bank of the Rhine, of course. In the long stretches of our separation, she was closer to me than in the few days each year when we saw each other. That night I felt her presence especially keenly. When I stood still, her image hopped three steps ahead and waited for me with open arms. When I shouted into the darkness a question as to whether I was the father of her child, she laughed out loud, so loud that I turned around to see if anyone was watching us. When a choking fear overcame me and I was close to leaping into the river, she tugged my sleeve in warning. Should I go to Budapest and ask for her hand, surrounded by her family, as would have been appropriate in the bourgeois Jewish circles her family belonged to? But what would happen if those circles refused my request? Maria had been prepared for a great musical career, not for a German composer of middling talent who put a bit of hard currency on the table to be allowed to take their daughter out of the country. And what if I was not the father of the child? If she only agreed to a fake marriage to give the child some security? And then off she would go to success in New York, while in my two-room apartment I would be teaching the child to play the violin, along with the basics of mathematics and perhaps Latin and physics? While the mother occasionally sent some clothes and a ticket every summer so the child could escape provincial Munich once a year? And in return I would be allowed to show the grandparents the Bavarian capital and listen to Strauss operas with them? And what if I did not really love her, but loved her only in the sad Warsaw Pact cities during the terrible music festivals, where I was desperate for love? And what if she did not love me anymore, but had only loved me in Budapest and Warsaw because she found my naiveté attractive in the context of such festivals?

In order to look my unhappiness in the eye, I sat down on a cold metal block, but it was too dark to see anything in the Rhine. Perhaps Maria was sitting on a wharf beside the Danube at the very same moment, thinking similar thoughts. Something had to happen, then; it didn't matter what.

I went back the way I had come. Because the fog had grown dense, I stumbled through puddles, fell down twice, and made a mess of my light trench coat, the one I had bought especially for the Cologne letdown. In any case, the people in the old-town bar I found still open did not see the rising young composer in me, but one of their own, and they greeted me amiably. A shape emerged from the dim background and approached me with his hand stuck out, a big fellow with long, honey-colored hair and narrow eyes. He took my hesitantly outstretched hand and pulled me to his table, ordered Kölsch and schnapps, and drew me into a conversation about music. He was also from Munich, he said, and knew me from demonstrations and discussions. That evening he had attended my concert, and been at the bar with the others afterward, but then he'd headed for the old town. In an unaffected, cheerful way, he told me of every insult I and my music had been subjected to in the conversation. It was what I would have expected, but I was still shocked and hurt. Nobody had taken my side, not even the musicians who, because of me, had been able to play a premiere—at which they had failed miserably. With your music, said Grützmacher, which was the fellow's name, you can't get anywhere right now; you're neither elitist nor popular; you don't have the right friends or the right enemies; you're not left-wing enough, but not emphatically aristocratic, either; your attitude is more defiant and protective than dynamic and aggressive; you don't want to close yourself off yet you don't want to belong, and so on. The worst of it is that it's so difficult to argue about your music! And that means in turn that reconciliation is impossible as well. You make the reconciliation that should follow being insulted impossible. Do you understand? What you're doing leads nowhere, he concluded in his friendly way. As for him, he had given up modern music and begun working with rock musicians; wonderful cats, as he put it. He had his own studio in Munich, where he produced music for Southwest German Television in Stuttgart, for the various series the one-armed actor from my building occasionally appeared in, the ones lonely Mrs. Köhler enjoyed so much. And then he thrust his card at me: the studio was in Grünwald, his apartment right above it. You've got to come see me, said Grützmacher. I'll show you how it's done. With me, you can earn a lot of cash without getting your fingers burned. We drank another Kölsch, and Grützmacher ran his hands through his mane before pulling a hundred-mark bill out of the top pocket of his jacket. He didn't bother with the change.

On seeing my mud-splashed coat, the night porter at the hotel asked for my name before handing me my key. Good night, I said at the elevator, but received no answer.

18

These days, memories of those years evoke a rage in me that nothing can mollify. I try to recall faces, names, hotel rooms, conversations. A memory tumor grows in my brain, a desire to touch everything and everyone one more time before all is erased from my mind forever. But the memories do not come into focus; they are blurry, distant. Sarajevo. Pierre Faye played Charles Ives. Was that in the National Library, in a wood-paneled room, or in the city hall? A poet gave the introduction, Ante or Anton, a drunken old man who moved mighty rhetorical backdrops and waved his arms as he talked about the partisans and their heroic struggle, which had laid the foundation for our being able to sit together in peace to hear music from the early years of the avant-garde. Suddenly he began to sing. In a loud voice, he sang a partisan song for us, suddenly a young man again in a long-lost time, the enemy before his closed eyes attacking and besieging him—but the old man, trembling all over, could only complete his song with the most extreme effort. Tears welling in his eyes, he bowed to the musicians, who clutched their instruments, stiff and embarrassed, and then he was escorted out like a strange animal after its circus performance. And as I remember the trembling partisan in his oversize suit being dragged out, I also remember that I remained motionless in my chair, my heart pounding, a man outraged and at a loss for words at the inappropriateness of the entire event. I could only stutter as I tried to convince Maria it was time to leave the room. But she stayed.

I left. I can't remember how I left the room, but I know for sure that the abruptness with which I got up and did it caused a commotion, because it wasn't clear whether I was leaving the concert because of Ante-or-Anton's drunken performance or because of Maria, who, when I was already at the heavy door, half rose to shout angrily at me, then sat down again. The notebook! Where is the red imitation-leather notebook, a gift from Maria, in which I was then in the habit of jotting down what I didn't want to forget? Ante-or-Anton's address and telephone number were in that notebook, at the top of a right-hand page. For I had only just left the National Library when the singer's strangely rocking form appeared in front of me. He was sunk in an exchange with himself, his arms making quick, fluttering gestures. After I had introduced myself, I recall, we went straight to a shashlik stand and had a conversation in bits and pieces of various languages over kebab and schnapps; that is, he told me his life story, every word of it a memorial only vaguely accessible to my memory now: Moscow, Lenin Prize, Cuba, Crimea, Tito, East Germany.

His ailing memory was further eroded by alcohol, and the words came out at irregular intervals. I remember a pale full moon over the mountains of Sarajevo, a skeptical companion with the thankless task of guiding us to the poet's apartment, which was at the edge of the city on the third floor of a high-rise. I remember ringing the bell because it was too embarrassing to ask the poet for the key, and a young woman opening the door—his daughter, as I later learned, whose name I also wrote down in my red notebook. But I cannot remember their family name. Where has that damn notebook gone?

We put the poet in his chair and settled at the dining room table; then the daughter told me her father's story again, with passionate conviction, this time in French instead of Italian. Later we went into the kitchen, but she kept running into the living room to get letters, books with dedications, and other sacred objects, which soon formed a wall between us. Father wants to die, she told me over the wall of fame and honor; he's almost there. He'll write one or two more poems, then he'll leave me. Because of the yoke of his memories, he can hardly move, and since my mother's death, I've been his substitute memory. I invent his life for him. I'm responsible for whether his end is triumphant. He's only a poet, you know. He's never done anything else. A Communist poet the Germans didn't manage to eliminate. An unstable existence. A lazybones who's hardly ever been happy. Two more poems, then he can lie in his grave of honor, and the old partisans will sing his favorite songs one more time. The complete edition of his poems is ready; if it doesn't come out right after his death, he'll be forgotten. That's our fate.

I remember sitting across from her at the little kitchen table. At some point, we heard the poet stumble through the hall to the toilet, then the silence returned, to be broken only by the daughter's fading voice.

I'll call you, I told her in the morning, and wrote Ante-or-Anton's name and hers in my red imitation-leather notebook. Out in the street, the sun, slowly creeping from balcony to balcony, had just reached hers. She waved as if from another world, and I was not sure if she was waving to me. I later wrote down the sad message of that wave, intending to make it the basis of a piece for piano and cello. For Ante-or-Anton. But what, for God's sake, was his daughter's name?

And where was that red notebook?

19

After our memorable encounter in Cologne, I started writing music for Grützmacher's shows, under a pseudonym, of course. I was amazed at how the money accumulated. Nothing flowed more easily from my hand than the right melody to accompany a society woman dead from an overdose or the accidentally murdered wife of an industrialist, and as the shows with my music were not only rebroadcast incessantly in Germany, Austria, and Switzerland, but also found friends and admirers in the rest of Europe, as well as in many other parts of the world, the till was ringing so deafeningly in my apartment that I could hardly find any peace and quiet for my serious work. Grützmacher was a genius at marketing, but still a friend, who retained one quarter and punctually paid the other three. For the first time in my life, accountants and investment bankers expressed an interest in the proceeds from my work, and even the tax man kept a critical eye on me. I could not afford to be squeamish when Grützmacher offered to sell me part of the company and proposed to make me vice president. Four times a year, we discussed the books with the tax lawyers and calculated the dividends; I learned to appreciate the value of writing off the new mixing boards; I drove a company car and before long had bought a larger apartment. Week after week, I tossed off a few feeble pieces of music for the detective shows and children's programs Grützmacher produced, and that was all it took for me to familiarize myself with capitalism's best side. Even when I had a meal with one of my few friends, the company paid the bill, to say nothing of the wine I drank in the evenings to get in the mood for murder mysteries. As Grützmacher had virtually no imagination, but was patently brilliant at running machines, the division of labor between us was quickly established. I wrote; he produced, negotiated, delivered. Most horrifying of all, we received national and international prizes for our shoddy efforts, which were always accepted by Grützmacher, who acquired a set of tuxedoes for the purpose at the company's expense. My theme songs for some of the popular talk shows became so popular that people whistled them on the street. And it stunned me when I heard my own works in the supermarket, arranged for strings in a way that obliterated any spark the originals might have had. As I did not own a television set, I was spared my music within my own four walls, and since I had no desire to leave my apartment, I was plagued by it only when ambushed in public places.

I heard little from Maria. A card told me she had given birth to a daughter. Someday you'll meet her, she wrote in squished letters in the margin, and you'll like her. The father's identity was not mentioned in the few letters she sent me after the birth of the highly praised child, though I never failed to take the opportunity to ask. Maria had married and divorced; another man had entered her life, a French opera director whose name I knew even though I had never seen anything directed by him. And when she had married and then separated from the director, she wrote to say that she hoped I would still be there for her. Her first husband had been a Hungarian pianist, the second the French director; obviously a trashy German composer was now the man to save her. Sometimes she performed in Germany, to rave reviews, but she gave Munich a wide berth. All I had of the child was a somewhat fuzzy photograph; all I had of Maria were memories. Sometimes I looked into the doll-like little girl's blurry button eyes to see whether I could find any resemblance to me, but with no tangible result. Half the white world could have been the father of that girl.

I did have a few affairs with women during these years, mostly musicians I met at Grützmacher's; they apparently hoped to help their careers by being with me. They rarely stayed after dinner, because they found my serious compositions, which I was in the habit of playing on the piano, unbearable. Sometimes, if they still saw light in the window, they would come back after the disco. They would lie down in my bed, only to have fallen asleep by the time I joined them at dawn. Embarrassingly enough, I could never remember their names. They came and went as I frittered away my life. Some could cook; most could only drink. When they said goodbye in the morning and I saw their faces above mine, already made up, hair done, an expression of maternal pity at my failed existence in their eyes, an uncontrollable hatred would rise in me, which I could only contain by quickly turning over onto my stomach. Still, whenever a Sylvie or a Tanja called in the evening and asked what I was up to, I would promptly ask her to join me for dinner.

Only one of these women was different, a Russian with a lovely, pear-shaped face who was on the verge of letting Grützmacher destroy her beautiful alto voice. She even stayed in the room while I played the piano, then read me Akhmatova and Mandelstam in the original before retiring into one of the back rooms as I stayed bent over my criminal melodies. When I came across her in the long corridor lined with bookshelves, where I paced up and down in search of inspiration, she would ask me in such a mournful voice whether I was sad that I would start to laugh. And you, I always responded, are you sad? She would shake her frizzy hair, dyed a different color every day, and sing a light, sun-drenched little song, and everything would seem fine.

Once, she asked me for ten thousand marks: she had a chance to bring her uncle from Kiev, who was over eighty, to the West. The handover was to take place in Passau. During the drive, with her knees drawn to her chest and her arms folded around them, she told me the story of her life and the story of her family, a sad narrative with many subplots that kept breaking off and starting anew, with no end in sight.

In the city, I had to wait in the car while she tramped off with a note in her hand. I saw her red hair vanish into the crowd like an innocent confidence and felt a solitude I had rarely felt before, a solitude that was a mixture of sorrow and shame. Suddenly I was startled by a gentle knock on the window, and when I turned to the side, scared to death, she was standing there with a timid-looking old man who was holding a battered suitcase and a briefcase. We were introduced with many bows; the two then got into the backseat, where they sat silent and motionless all the way to Munich. Once I felt her hand on the back of my head, but just as I reached for it, it vanished into the darkness behind me.

The money was paid back in ten installments; I never saw the girl again. Even Grützmacher had no idea where she was. All she left was her question. Sometimes as I walk past the bookshelves in the corridor, I ask myself: Are you sad? And then I sing a little song on my way back to the kitchen.

Another of my relationships was with a real admirer. She considered herself a painter and had decided that she wanted to illustrate my music. She traveled to the few concerts where my music was performed, asked for autographs, and talked about what my music meant to her in such an excited and friendly way that, after a while, I had no choice but to invite her to the meals I had after the performances. Some colleagues thought we were married and, when she was late, asked me where my wife was. Her name was Sonya; she was big and strong and had a tremendous head of blond hair that terrified me because it reminded me of my mother's. On top of everything else, she got it into her head that she wanted to paint my portrait, and eventually I agreed to sit for her for a day. She came from

Karlsruhe with two suitcases, walked into my apartment like a victorious general, and in no time had given the wilted atmosphere of my rooms an artificial cheerfulness by draping something here and tying something there, strategically distributing the flowers she had brought, putting wine bottles on the bookshelves, and generally behaving as if she wanted to spend the rest of her life there. When she had finished her preparations for the portrait, I put on tapes of my music, which she needed for inspiration. Then she insisted that I try on other clothes, various shirts and the six pairs of pants I had accumulated over time, which exposed me to her scrutiny. Now jump to it, she said as I tried to slip into my pants in such a way that neither a direct look nor a glance at the mirror would reveal any part of me I didn't want observed, but when she commented on my clownish distortions by saying she was going to buy me some new underwear, my already weakened resistance was destroyed. The more I refused to interact with her, the stronger her concern became, and the silence I sank into gave her loquaciousness an unexpected energy. Her crazy actions somehow made me compliant, though. For example, she did not shrink from touching my body—to be precise, she touched my belly with the flat of her hand to recommend the proper breathing technique for the long sitting sessions—the adequate breathing technique, as she put it, because we don't want you to suddenly slide out of your chair, do we? And with that statement in the plural, her hand intentionally lingered between solar plexus and pubic area for so long that my senses actually did threaten to swoon. But her primary weapon was only employed when I sat down, as if dead, in my armchair and she grew deceptively quiet, her drawing pad on her stool. Suddenly she stood up, cursing angrily. That's not you, she shouted at me. I see a broken-down sissy, a despicable weakling, not an artist, not a musician, nothing outstanding, nothing deep, nothing metaphysical! Look at me now, she said threateningly, as I tried to focus my gaze on my shoes, and what I had been anticipating for hours with the greatest pain in my soul then happened: She took one comb after another out of the overwhelming beehive of hair and put them between her bared teeth, crossed her arms to grab the hem of her sweater, and flung it over her head and into the air. With a dismayed expression, as if looking at an infectious disease, I saw my mother before me as I had never seen her and had never been allowed to see her: nude. God knows how she had removed all the items of clothing that usually protect a woman so quickly; in any case, there she was sitting opposite me in a way that made me think I should be the one to reach for the drawing pad and the charcoal. But that was unthinkable. I squatted in my chair, in my best suit, petrified and embittered, while the woman from Karlsruhe, who was married to a minor industrialist, department of mechanical engineering, monopolist, busied herself drawing powerful lines on the sketchpad on her wide-open thighs and saying, Soon we'll have it, soon it'll be done. I was not allowed to move; I was not allowed to turn on the light. The objects in the room briefly awakened, then fell asleep again, and the house sank deep into shadows and brooding. Eventually the sketchpad was used up, the sitting over. We won't get anything else done today, the woman sighed, exactly as my mother used to sigh. As I was incapable of getting up in this exceptional situation, I let her drag me out of the chair and into the bathroom, where she quickly washed and undressed me, then basically carried me to bed. Everything else became the property of the night. The portrait was finished in a week. The man it depicted looked like a turtle fearfully sticking its head out of its shell. Whoever looked closely could find a naked woman with heavy breasts in the dark background, raising her arms as if to cast a spell. The muse, said the woman from Karlsruhe. She was pleased: My best painting. It was not for sale; otherwise, I could have let it rot in the attic. Luckily, though, one could not tell from the painting how it was made, and besides, it was our secret, the painter's and mine, that she had mixed certain secretions into the paint, for magical purposes. When, years later, I read in a magazine that an American artist used menstrual blood as paint, for conceptual reasons, it made me think of my Karlsruhe admirer, who at least in this sense had to be considered a member of the avant-garde. After a week, she vanished, along with her painting, from my life. I later heard from artist friends that she always employed such techniques to help with her portraits, until eventually she stumbled on a sculptor who, after being molested for three days, beat her so badly she had to go to the hospital. He was found not guilty.

Besides such fleeting relationships, I had little to distract me. I was barely interested in either the rapid and scarcely innovative development of art or in the development of society. I read a lot, composed a lot, loafed around a lot. Was I happy? Or was I sad?

20

A week after Judit's party ended, and two days after her mother's departure, it was impossible for me to visualize Maria's face. At times I felt that I had not seen her at all. Her hair, her eyes, her wide-open arms and her embrace, after I had completed the endless journey through the honor guard of Hungarians to her, the smell of her hair, the color of her dress—yes, there were details, but they did not add up to a person, a human being. The other Maria, the one from more than twenty years ago, stood more clearly before me than the strange woman who had just been running around my apartment, always a touch too loud, as if taking possession of it, as if the sheet music, the books, and the piano belonged to her, as if she had sent her daughter as a stand-in to stop the frightening decay of her beloved objects. The Hungarians still in the apartment—Uncle Sandor, Janos, and two children whose origin could not be precisely determined—kept a respectful distance, because they were apparently used to such performances from her. Uncle

Sandor smoked in front of the television and was scolded for it; Janos tenaciously read a commentary on the Talmud; the two children, a girl of about fourteen and a little boy she controlled like a slave, had retired to my library and were reading, syllable by syllable, the captions in an illustrated history of erotic painting from the Stone Age to the present. Who are you, I asked the children a couple of times when Maria was out of hearing, as they wandered through the apartment wearing next to nothing. Leave the children alone, Judit hissed. They don't belong to you; you don't have to grab everything that moves. Had the children been left behind? Even the uncle and Janos, whom I asked about the children's origins behind the backs of the women, were unable to provide much information. Their father's name was Miklós, their mother's Magda, but the children could not say where their parents were at present, even after repeated questioning in Hungarian.

Maria went shopping; Maria had an appointment at the hairdresser's; Maria had a mask put on to prevent the wrinkles likely to appear after parties; Maria had long telephone conversations in various languages with the entire world. But her principal activity in the days of her stay in my apartment consisted of long conversations with Judit, from which, naturally, I was excluded. I heard loud laughter and nasty squealing, gurgling attacks of tears and comforting persuasion; every register available to a great singer was pulled. But why, what for?

On the second day after the party, my appetite for leftovers had faded, and I made a date with Günter, hoping to recover with the help of a private conversation in German.

I was at the door, the handle to freedom in my hand, when Judit angrily charged toward me down the dark hall.

Where are you going? she shouted.

I'm going to have a working dinner with Günter, I responded. I was telling the truth, but she noticed, from the odd ease with which this statement passed my lips, that it was not the whole truth.

And you'll let your guests here go hungry?

While she spoke, the door to the room where she had been closeted with Maria was being pushed open, slowly, and a thin strip of light was forming on the wooden floor of the hall.

I understand that you prefer fleeing to taking my mother and me out, but I wouldn't have expected you to let Uncle Sandor and Janos and those two half-wild children starve.

There are plenty of leftovers in the pantry, I said, lamely.

Yes, my relatives can dig through the garbage, she screamed, so loudly that all the Hungarians in my household stepped out of their rooms into the hall and stared at me—the man with his hand on the doorknob.

Good, then we'll all go together, I surrendered, and, except for Maria and Judit, all the others obediently came along to the restaurant, Mario's, where Mario himself, after introductions, told the uncle and Janos that once, years ago, he had been in love with a Hungarian woman whose erotic tendencies had left nothing to be desired.

It turned into one of those artist evenings I hate so much. Günter played the writer who was well known but whose true importance had not yet been fully recognized, the uncle smoked, Janos said not a word, and the two children fell asleep in my lap after the appetizer, which prevented me from eating my spaghetti like a civilized person.

We got home around eleven o'clock, accompanied by Günter, who was carrying the boy in his arms, neither of the children's two countrymen being capable of such an effort. I had the girl wrapped around my shoulders; she was quietly babbling to herself and occasionally humming a little song in a trembling voice. Odd burden. I was now providing accommodations for three generations of Hungarians in my apartment, where I was still tolerated, albeit with a limited residence permit.

We opened the apartment door. It was suspiciously dark. With the girl on my shoulders it was impossible for me to enter and feel for the light switch, and Günter had already accidentally bumped the boy's head on the railing, so, as Uncle Sandor had a pathological fear of the dark and was sitting on the steps breathing hard, Janos had to take over the task of casting some light on a situation that was getting ever darker.

The two women had gone out. I can't say I was disappointed; on the contrary, some of the old coziness, the familiarity, returned when, after taking care of the two children, we four men sat down at the round table in the kitchen to discuss the absent women in peace. Günter, especially, who could be both excitable and quarrelsome, was able to get the two Hungarian friends to provide so many details about Maria and the way she lived that in the course of the night the love affair in which I had played the lead role, until then a monumental epic, was edited down to a short story heading toward its inevitable denouement. As I now heard for the first time, Maria had been a member of the party, something she had always denied, and she had been a member when we met. Hence, the secret police had known about her affair with me from the start, which must have led to the inevitable consequences. Janos, who knew all this and enjoyed telling the story, and Sandor, who also knew all this but was more discreet, outdid each other—inspired by a first-class grappa Mario had sold us at an unconscionable price—in providing details of how, in Maria's life, a love of music had become a love of ideology, which led Günter, when it was already past two o'clock, to ask the decisive question, with a drunkenly leering expression: In light of everything, must I not be Judit's father? A profound silence conquered the room. Only the uncle's pipe could be heard.

Until then, my life had not cast any real shadows. I had been the quiet fool, good at this and that, free of envy and excessive ambition. I had remained more or less faithful to my eccentric love of socialism, although I now voted for one of those parties in Germany with social-democratic inclinations: the rich should get richer so the poor do not have to get poorer. In the universe of the given facts, I had found myself a tiny spot where I lived and worked: some music and a few books. Everything I had done was done discreetly, as used to be the custom in West Germany. I had never competed for anything, or, to be precise, I never had to compete for anything. The need to express myself was alien to me; I had always tried to avoid excesses of vitality. Perhaps my deceptively harmless appearance was a sign of stupidity; perhaps one had to be present at decisive occasions, like Günter, who had been at the New Year's reception of the Bavarian prime minister—the minister had never thought to invite me—at the chancellor's monthly gathering of artists, at the president's social gatherings. Perhaps one had to be a member of the Writers Union, on the advisory board of the Goethe Institute, in the Humboldt Society, on the union's cultural subcommittee, involved in the foundations sponsored by Mercedes or Siemens or Müller Bread. All I had ever tried to do was figure myself out as discreetly as possible, and that had been more than enough to keep me busy my whole life. The idea that I, of all people, was supposed to have fallen in love with Maria under the patronage of the Hungarian secret police and fathered her child was so absurd that I answered Günter's insinuation with a laugh. Remote conception, I exclaimed. You don't believe in remote conception, do you? And while I refilled the grappa glasses, the sleepy little Hungarian girl came into the kitchen and asked for a glass of water.

When the girl left, so did the uncle and Janos, and so did Günter—usually the last person to voluntarily leave behind a bottle not yet empty. I went downstairs and waited with him for his taxi. Just before he took off, he dealt me yet another blow with his last observation: probably the uncle and Janos had been working for the secret police as well; otherwise, how would they have known the details of how Maria had betrayed my love for her?

Wasn't I a member of the conspiracy, too? I shouted after him, but the taxi had already sped off.

I was standing in the street, brooding, indecisive about how to act toward the troop of Hungarian spies in my apartment, when another taxi came up from the other direction. Probably Günter, I thought, with no money in his pockets. But it was Judit. She was alone. Maria, she told me, had decided to spend the last night before her departure at the Four Seasons Hotel, safe from me and Uncle Sandor and Janos, who all seemed like judges to her. I was the judge; the two Hungarian friends were the assessors. But if she's innocent, what does she have to be afraid of, I asked. Who can still claim to be innocent these days? said Judit. You least of all; anyway, you've been drinking.

We walked around the block to get some fresh air. I suggested going to France right after the uncle and Janos had left. For the next three days, I'll go into the studio; then we can disappear. In France, I'll start the Mandelstam opera, if you let me work.

But the departure took a bit longer than that. First, the children's parents were hard to find, and when we had finally found them—in Paris—they didn't want to come back right away. Only with effort could I prevent Maria from personally delivering the children to Paris, as real friends supposedly would have done. So it was good that the rest of the family, the uncle and Janos, did not feel the least desire to see their homeland again, and the prospect of being allowed to make use of the television all alone put the uncle in a positively enthusiastic mood, while my friend Janos was utterly elated by the idea of being able to use the library without having to talk to anyone. Large quantities of milk were bought for the children, and boxes of noodles for the adults; in long meetings, the cleaning lady was told what quantities and kinds of meals to prepare; Sandor was warned to keep close track of the sparks flying from his pipe; Janos what to do in case of fire; the children, who by then were on the verge of going totally wild, received anthologies of Hungarian poetry from Judit, in place of the history of erotic painting, along with a wealth of instructions on how to behave until their parents returned. Then my car was loaded to the roof—and, certain that I would never again see my apartment, or at least not in a recognizable state, I drove with Judit to France. By the time we got to the border that separates Munich from Bavaria, I was imagining Janos studying my letters from Maria, which were stored in a secret compartment of my desk; I was imagining Uncle Sandor watching an episode of his beloved *Searchers* on Channel 1, with my music, while the curtains burned; I was imagining the children wrestling in the stairwell, half-naked, which would lead to charges being filed. My downfall was fixed in my mind's eye by the time we reached Bregenz; I had a premonition of the end of my bourgeois existence as we left Switzerland; I knew that now I would have to actually begin to work when we spent the night in Nîmes. I was happy—indeed, in a state of infantile bliss—when my French house came into view. I had arrived.

21

We had barely finished unpacking the car when first the house and then the garden were turned on their heads. Judit administered her talent for making herself unloved prudently. The fact that a house one had never entered before could be turned upside down amazed me. Everything had to be moved around, changed. At once! In Judit's opinion, for which she provided no justification, I had to give the garden a makeover so it would mirror the house. A makeover! In fact, the garden did look run-down, random, and overgrown; the beautiful views were blocked by never-pruned bushes that had grown lushly and were overrun by parasites, creepers, and burdocks. I had bought the house ten years before and done nothing since then but put in an herb garden. I liked the rawness of the vegetation, the tangled confusion that surrounded the clean lines of the building, with its pale sandstone blocks. I liked the thick ivy that covered large parts of the walls, even if it threatened to tear off the gutters. And I was besotted with the wild roses that resisted every attempt to fence them in. In this labyrinth that scorned everything about the civilized art of gardening, this unplanned paradise of plants, and animals dozing in the shelter provided by the crumbling walls, in magnificently empty hours, I had had my greatest inspirations. Smoking in a creaking wicker chair, I had watched sunsets reddening the wide sky and wisps of cloud drawn on the horizon with a broad stroke, had jotted thoughts down in a notebook on my thorn-scratched knees, thoughts that seemed definitive and pure, untouched by goals and clear intentions. How different they were from the chaotic, confused notebooks of my urban existence! But I had also worked on my compositions in this garden and in the friendly house, in the large, cool room on the ground floor, often all night and into the morning hours, when the birds began to chirp in the hedges and I would shut the windows and lie down on the iron bed to sleep. No house or apartment in a city can evoke such a triumphant feeling of happiness. I was lucky, as I have been all too rarely in my life. For this house, along with its hopeless disorder, was my place. Nobody had ever interfered with it. None of the visitors who stopped by for a few days in the summer on their way to Provence or the seaside, nor any of the guests who often stayed for weeks, had ever infringed on the unwritten house rule, the law of this property: Don't change anything!

And now I saw myself, the guardian of that law, which had survived for ten years, turn the order on its head. I acted as my own lawbreaker. Allegedly harmful creepers were removed; bushes that blocked the view into the valley uprooted; two little trees that had grown in my garden of their own accord were cruelly and ruthlessly felled, and the tall trees were trimmed, especially the almond tree, the hedges were pruned, the potted plants moved—when they were shown any mercy at all. I spent all day with hoe, saw, and spade, as if I had to make up for ten years of neglect in a week. I felt awful and had a bad conscience, yet I quickly succumbed to the exhilaration of cutting, pruning, and eradicating; often, I had to pause, breathing hard, to spare the garden my fury. In the evenings, while Judit made dinner, I would sit in my wicker chair, my limbs aching, and look anxiously at the bare scene. I was now able to scan the hills rising up on the other side of the valley. In the distance, in the dry, shimmering light, dense green woods lay like exhausted animals; at the edge of the yellow fields, houses sent smoke signals and tiny cars floated through the thin branches as if pulled by strings. The world beyond the garden was now visible, and I was visible to the world. I was horrified the first time I saw my neighbor on his tractor, and he saw me: a bent man in a wicker chair, waiting in the dusk for his supper. My last supper, I suddenly thought, and got up at once and headed to the kitchen on legs covered with mosquito bites; at least I could get my food myself.

Judit was by and large satisfied with my work: You have to prune the hedge some more here; these plants have to go in the shade, because they don't tolerate sun; we have to put in a gravel path between the house and the wall, with a table and chairs at the end, so we can eat there in the evening and have a view of the valley. My work was slowly approaching her idea of a Mediterranean garden, an idea she had picked up entirely from books. Judit had never been in France before.

After ten days of uninterrupted drudgery, I wanted to begin composing, so as to get down a few of the ideas that had germinated during the unfamiliar physical labor, but Judit implored me to put the house in order first. Otherwise, one day we'll get here and find a ruin, she said. We? Why we? But I fell into line, drove to Nevac, and came back with a carload of paint and brushes. In another week, all the woodwork—doors and window frames— was painted gray; the heavy beams that supported the roof treated against woodworms; the wasps' nests removed; three laborers, who shared lunch with us, had dug and built a well because the tap water I loved to drink was suppos- edly full of pesticides; all the cracks in the walls, which I had viewed vaguely as a mystery, had been filled with concrete; the wooden front door torn out and replaced. Even the in- nocent moles that left the sounds of their wild music in the grass were brutally banished. We were to stay, everything else had to go. Judit completed the job by hiring a carpen- ter to build shelves, on which she put the books in reason- able order, something I had never succeeded in doing; the old dishes were replaced by new ones she picked up "for nothing" at the secondhand shop, along with some old em- broidered bedspreads. My mattresses, sagging horsehair monstrosities, were sent to the dump. How can we sleep on these mattresses? she asked. You walk like an old man, bent, in pain. So we bought mattresses that were better for our spines, and if they were to have any beneficial effect, new pads and frames were in order. You have to think of your old age, said Judit one evening when, peacefully, for a change, we were sitting on the terrace marveling at the sunset. I won't always be able to take care of you. I may be able to come by between concerts, but the rest of the time you'll have to get by on your own. She was thinking about hiring a woman from the village to do the cooking and gardening for me, an old woman who would not distract me. I'm fifty, I said, and until now I've got along better on my own than with anyone else.

Yes, she said, and in ten years you'll be sixty, an old man who loves red wine and lives off of a few pieces of kitschy television music and occasionally leafs through the yellowed sheets of chamber music he still believes to be better than any of the newer things, a man who pins up an old opera poster by the toilet so he can read his own name twice a day. And when you're sixty, I'll be thirty-two, playing Ligeti and Kurtag, both of whom are seventy today and will then be eighty and will still be talked about, because they believed in their music and worked hard. But it's doubtful whether I'll still have the desire and the time, at thirty-two, to take care of an old cynic who sits in his dilapidated house in France and watches the lizards racing past his bare feet.

And before I could respond to her pathetic barrage, she had vanished into my house (which was not dilapidated at all), where before long I heard her playing the cello.

Tomorrow, I'll begin working on my Mandelstam opera, I thought, irritated, and she'll have to take care of the house by herself. The long S-curve of the road on the hill opposite shone like a warning. A car drove down the hill, leaving behind a thin dust cloud that hung in the air for a while. It was past ten o'clock, time to go to bed, so I could be up early to work on my music.

I crept around the house to the front entrance so Judit would not notice I was going to bed. At our new well, I splashed my face with two handfuls of water (still warm), then I opened the door like a thief and tiptoed up the wooden stairs. Judit continued to practice. In my underwear, I lay down on the new mattress, pulled the sheet up, rolled onto my side, and listened. We all have hidden gardens and plantations in ourselves, I thought, but I could not hold on to the thought. Judit was too close. Her presence made all independent thought impossible.

She was probably right. I would probably be lying in exactly the same position ten years from now, listening to the evening sounds while she raced from concert to concert, performing. Every three weeks, I would get a postcard summarizing the latest triumphs, which I would pin on the wall over the kitchen sink. Once a year, I would take her out to dinner after a concert in Munich; heads would turn to look at her, and everyone would wonder whether I was her father or her agent. And, with a laugh, they would ask if I would write a piece for her, but something beautiful, free. A ghastly rage suffused my body, then turned into fierce hatred. She might well break her hand tomorrow or fall off her bicycle or poison herself with the berries she picked and stuffed into her mouth. Then she will ask for my help. But I will not give it! I will reject her pleas with malice, the same malice with which she attacked me. I will treat her like an abandoned lover; I will be a stranger to her; she will not recognize me.

At that moment, she called my name; she called it questioningly: György? She had got into the habit of pronouncing my name Hungarian-fashion when she wanted to be especially sweet. György? I held my breath. Through the cracks in the floorboards, I could see her wandering shadow; then I heard her softly whistling as she put the cello away; I heard the latches snap shut and the muffled sound of the case being placed in the corner. Again: György? No, I am not here for her anymore. Now she will go to the telephone, I thought, and call her mother, and in fact, I did hear her dial the old-fashioned dial, a lot of numbers. Maria? she asked after an endless wait, followed by a long conversation in Hungarian, in which my name came up every few seconds. Jealousy made me sweat when she giggled: György? *Kekmatchmögvatalassam.* On and on it went until she signed off with a whispered *Servus.*

What was I to do? Since I could not get the better of her with friendliness, I would have to fan the flames of my hatred. Hatred drives the enemy out of his hiding place; friendliness makes him hold fast. Maybe I should just throw her out of the house?

Judit's bed was downstairs in the guest room, by the kitchen. I deduced from the sound of the crunching gravel that she was walking around the house and, for reasons I could not fathom, closing the shutters; then she came back inside and went into the bathroom through the squeaking door. I heard the flushing of the toilet. Then another door opened, which I could not identify. And as I tried to collect myself so I could finally get some sleep after all the evening's affronts, she appeared on the edge of my bed.

Are you asleep? she asked.

No, I said, I'm thinking.

And what does a man think about at midnight?

Nothing.

Are you a Buddhist, who can think about nothing?

No, I said, I'm a Christian in love with fatigue, wondering what sins he committed to have the twenty-two-year-old daughter of a Hungarian friend torment him so.

I simply told you the truth, she said. And Maria agrees with me. I should take care of you; otherwise, you'll fall apart. You should be writing.

How am I supposed to be writing, Judit, when I am digging up the garden from morning till night, painting window frames, digging wells, and putting up with insults?

You weren't writing in the city, either. You sit around all day long with books and nothing happens; that's the truth.

There is no truth, I said. That's written in the books.

If nonsense like that is in your books, you shouldn't read them. There is truth in art, after all.

That's nice, I said wearily, but it's hidden behind many masks.

Then it's your duty to draw it out. With your music.

But nobody wants to hear that music, I shouted angrily, that is the truth. My Mandelstam opera will have three performances in Nuremberg, if the producer lasts, and that'll be that.

You're as whiny as a small child, said Judit, stroking my hand, which lay on the white sheet like an unfamiliar

brown animal. And besides, Mandelstam's the wrong subject. You should have written a Mandelstam opera twenty
years ago, when you met my mother. That would've been
revolutionary. But today? Today it's too easy to put something on the Nuremberg Opera stage to mourn a poet
murdered by Stalin.

I don't want to mourn him, Judit; I want to hold him
up as an example.

Hold him up then, said Judit, and make sure he doesn't
fall over.

At some point in that long night, when it was getting
light outside and the birds were beginning to stir, I sat up,
covered with sweat, my eyelids burning, and shouted, my
arms stretched out pathetically: I want to sleep! I'm in my
house, which I bought with my own hard-earned money,
and I have the right, at three in the morning, after a long
day of labor, to sleep! —If, after all this talk, I can sleep at
all, I added, exhausted by self-pity.

Of course you'll be able to sleep, György, said Judit,
then lay down beside me on the bed, put both her hands
over my eyes, and softly sang a Hungarian lullaby, to which
I succumbed at once. Not even the mosquito flying in
circles around my head bothered me. Come and get *your*
drop of blood, I whispered.

22

When I woke up next to an unusually warm body and looked at the clock, it was six-thirty. My life had changed dramatically.

I slipped out of bed, embarassed. Judit's naked body, her arms, which suddenly reached into thin air, then slithered back to her sides, her oddly twisted legs twitching gently in her sleep—this picture of a girl, at whom I gaped voyeuristically, was anything but innocent.

I crept downstairs to the kitchen, made coffee, sat in my wicker chair in the garden, and tried to think things over. The world still lay behind a thin screen, which was being lifted bit by bit to expose it to the sun. The lizards were out and about, a pair of butterflies wobbled past, the birds greeted me with insults because I had cut their hedge down, and streams of ants, heavily laden and unconcerned by the night's events, walked nervously past my bare feet. I was just about to pull a thread out of the thick tangle of the night's conversation when Judit appeared in the door, a fogged-up glass of cold milk in her hand. Let's go for a walk, she said, before it gets too hot. It doesn't make any sense to think about yesterday.

I'm not thinking, I'm dreaming, I said. But I joined her anyway.

There were several farmhouses on the crest of the hill, from which we headed west into the next valley. A dog must have followed us from one of them, a hunting dog of a breed common here. He was walking in front of us, a black-and-white animal whose head was divided into a white half and a black half. His body was sprinkled with red flea powder. I liked that dog and fancied he had followed us because of me. I threw sticks, hid behind a tree, and was delighted when he stopped, bewildered, to look for me. I called him Osip to annoy Judit, who thought we should send him back. Go home! she shouted, clapping her hands aggressively, but the dog, who clearly had considerable experience in physical punishment, just looked from her to me, waved its disheveled tail, and trotted on. Good Osip. We'll take the animal back on our way home, I said, and I enjoyed saying "the animal." At a mill in the valley, we could see two black dogs from a long way off. Judit wanted to turn around when the two started moving and barking; I went on. Osip will protect us, I said. But Osip was nowhere to be seen. Osip had made himself scarce, left us to our fate, which did not look rosy, for the two black monsters blocked our path, growling and baring their teeth, leaping at us, panting, and keeping us in check as we stood there in the middle of the path, pressed against each other. Finally, the miller arrived and whistled through his teeth; we were both conquered and saved.

You coward, said Judit, annoyed, to Osip when the dog joined us again behind the mill. I kept waiting for further commentary, but none was forthcoming. We stopped to rest under an almond tree. I stretched on the ground to smoke, my friend lay beside me panting, the black side of his head facing me. You're just like that dog, said Judit. You avoid the decisive tests.

I said nothing. I thought about that half-hour I had overslept. I would probably never make up for it.

What Judit had foreseen came to pass. Osip stayed with us all the way home, lapped up the water I scooped out of the well for him, and with no sign of feeling out of place, lay down under the table, on which I spread out my papers to start working.

I'll walk the dog back tomorrow, I said to Judit. Let me take care of a friend under my roof for a day, someone who feels comfortable here.

I had several notebooks in which I had compiled facts about life in the Soviet Union that might be relevant to my opera, from the Kirov assassination to the end of the Second World War. One notebook, the yellow one, contained notes about life in the Soviet camps. In fact, I had been surprised to find how few accounts existed; they were meager compared to the documentation about German camps. Of course, in the countries where Communist parties still had followers, reports about Soviet camps were not eagerly read or discussed. That made sense. Who wants to be told his house is built on bones? I found nothing worth noting, then, in the French and Italian party literature. Even when it was acknowledged that something had happened, that the mourning of several million people had simply been ignored, it was only in abstract statements. Other peoples deal with memory even more indifferently than we do. There was hardly a trace of the pain, which always takes time to sink into a people's consciousness. Even so, in the course of time I succeeded in collecting and analyzing a few hundred pages, though I often found it difficult to copy down the facts. Sometimes I would cut passages out of photocopies and glue them into the yellow notebook because I was unable to record the monstrosities with my own hand. The more thoroughly I studied the camp system, the harder it became for me to imagine music that could provide even a distant echo of such suffering. Unlike in Germany, where those declared responsible for the national catastrophe had been identified early in the process, the people tormented in the Soviet camps were friends, members of a party one side of which had declared the other an enemy to justify its own misdeeds. It was curious that, according to the reports, the comrades who were declared enemies did not feel they were enemies of the Soviet Union; even at the time of their deepest humiliation, they wanted to be treated merely as enemies of the party—that is, they recognized their punishment without accepting their guilt. Did they hope, then, to be able to reestablish themselves in society after life in the camp? Was their recognition of the camp a survival strategy, because nobody who was ever in the camp could expect to find a different social system when they got out? What did an artist like Mandelstam think? What did the others think, who had just got a call from Stalin asking how they were? Did they believe that after they completed their sentences they would be embraced and accepted again? None of the lords of culture and faith who starved, were shot, or were otherwise dispensed with in the camps had taken part in counterrevolutionary activity; none had shouted "Down with Stalin!" in the Moscow Metro or handed out flyers in Red Square; none of the German Communists in Moscow had secretly supported the Social Democrats—no, they were all believers, and they were tortured to death by believers, by their own kind.

And Mandelstam?

I tried to organize the notes. It had to be possible to find an organizing principle so minimally organized that it would encompass reality. Only through the total absence of the camp on the stage could the camp be represented.

Under the heading "Writing utensils," I had put all the reports dealing with writing, with getting paper and pencils, and with the attempts to jot down notes in the margins of letters or on medicine labels from the sick bay. This category also included a list of every mention of poets or poems, as well as reports of a camp university where lectures were held on French literature, or on Pushkin and Goncharov, often for just a single student. A second section was titled "Culture and games," and included references to evenings of music, as well as to chess games played with handmade pieces. Further, I had introduced a heading called "Scenes," where I collected testimonies of cruelty: in some camps, the refusal to work was not punished by immediate execution but by forcing the delinquent to stand at night in snow and ice until he either submitted or died. This section also contained the many reports about night and sleep: from the whispered prayers to the screams of prisoners tormented by nightmares. Above all, "Prayers": this section included the most fervent imaginable conversations with God, long mystical tirades reported by people who sat beside a dying inmate who prayed until the moment of his death. I had already worked out one scene a little. Because the state had abolished all Christian and Jewish holidays and made them punishable offences, they were observed in secret. In my scene, a group of prisoners prepares a holiday dinner—a piece of bread and a bowl of hot water—while someone recites poems, then they exchange gifts, with the nonsmoker giving the smoker a butt, who in turn gives a button to a comrade whose pants keep falling down, etc., until at the end they join in prayer. A pitiful, horrifying, but sublime scene of how, in such abysses, survival becomes possible.

Once the five notebooks were filled with my compact scrawl, I was overcome by such a wrenching feeling of shame that, although they were my only connection to the Osip Mandelstam I lionized so (except for his poems, which I could only read in translation), I would have liked to burn them—as the only sacrifice I could make in his memory. The sentences I had written, the confessions I had reaffirmed by jotting them down, the illnesses I had looked up to understand what they were—that extreme lunacy had destroyed my thinking to such a degree that at times I was unable to touch the notebooks. And still the humiliation emitted a disgusting, unconquerable fascination, one that made me pick up my documentation again and again: "When I returned to Poland, I could not find a single one of my relatives alive. My entire family, every near and distant relative, was dead. And in those sleepless nights I longed for someone to understand me, someone who had also been in a Soviet work camp.... It was not easy back then to establish my position as leader in the construction brigades. In Russia, you know, one has to pay for everything. In February 1942, about a month after I was transferred to the technicians' barracks, I was arrested by the NKVD. It was the period when the Russians went through the camps avenging their defeats on the front. There were four Germans in my brigade, two who came from the Volga region and were Russified, and two communists who had fled to Russia in 1935. They were good workers, and I had nothing against them, except perhaps that they avoided all political discussion like the plague. So the NKVD put a statement before me in which I supposedly claimed that I had heard these men talking in German about how Hitler would be coming soon. I was to confirm the correctness of this accusation with my signature. Oh God, one of the great nightmares of the Soviet system was surely the madness of wanting to liquidate its victims through legal procedures. It is not enough to put a bullet through somebody's head; no, he has to be made to ask for it in court. It was not enough for them to accuse somebody of an act he never committed; they also had to have witnesses to swear he did it. The NKVD left me no doubt that, if I refused to sign this paper, I would have to work in the forest again.... I had to choose between my own death and the deaths of the four men.... I chose. I had had enough of the forest and the gruesome daily struggle with death—I wanted to live. I signed. Two days later the men were shot outside the camp."

23

While she relentlessly rejected most people, Judit was neutral to all animals—except Osip—that sought shelter with us. Within a short time, more animals lived on my property than I would have liked, for I was the one who had to intervene in their occasionally violent confrontations. It was impossible to get Judit to say, for example, why we had to raise magpies that had fallen out of their nests. Daylight robbers, I'd say, when I had to put the worms she had chopped up into their wide-open beaks. Even the cats that joined us were not all innocents, as Judit claimed. In the morning, they sat hissing by the cadavers of the mice they had killed, and once they were sated, they left the disgusting remains on the kitchen floor. Only the hedgehogs behaved acceptably. They could not be rattled by the screaming of the birds or the rude and cowardly attacks of the dogs, who envied them their meager meal and their tiny bowl of milk. Even the snails that eagerly annihilated the vegetable garden were not thrown over the fence into the neighbor's yard, say, as I had been accustomed to doing in my youth; in-

stead, they were put in an old, barred crib behind the com-
post pile, and I had to feed them leftover noodles. Once a
week, the mailman picked them out of the muck and took
them home to fry in garlic oil.

Judit was a child of civilization in every respect. She
came from a family who considered everything civilized
especially important, and how she became attached to nature here in the countryside remained a riddle to me. Not
that she ever stopped complaining about how the beasts
robbed her of the time she needed for art, which she still
valued above the animals. Clearly, she was able to relate to
different worlds and could survive effortlessly in different
systems. But not in art, to which she applied sacred stan-
dards. Her tirades against anything inartistic sometimes
sounded like a page out of the Old Testament, which was
ridiculous coming from such a young person. She fired accusations at the post office for having chosen a ghastly design for stamps; she explained to the bewildered village
mayor, in great detail, why he should remove the fountain
specially built by a not very talented but nonetheless in-
genious artist from Toulouse—it did not complement the
houses around the market square; she recast the tobac-
conist's window, against his initially vehement resistance,
by relegating the decorations on display there to the garbage dump. She maintained that people could only call
themselves human if they surrounded themselves with
beautiful objects. And she was the one who determined
what was beautiful. I admit that French stamps might not
exemplify the best in art, that the modernist fountain did,
in fact, look ghastly amid the houses of pale brick, and that
Monsieur Aubric's tiny display window had not provided

an opportunity to contemplate beauty. What startled me was the total intolerance with which she pursued these issues. On the one hand, there was nature, which had to be admired, defended, and saved; on the other, there was the religion of art, whose rites had to be observed unconditionally. We saved Monsieur Aubric, she claimed, while M. Aubric watched us with an irate expression as we left behind his now almost empty display window. She did not care whether the poor man had wanted to be saved, or whether his customers, who had felt at home in his gloomy cage, would now switch to the supermarket.

Someone with so many mutually exclusive alternatives at her disposal had to be a quick-change artist. Perhaps she didn't yet have a sense of her true self. Or was she simply showing me all her masks, as if she were a mannequin, so I could understand her once and for all?

But I held my tongue.

The prevailing feeling I had had over the years was one of emptiness, a pleasant emptiness that caressed the body, an unfurnished space where anything was possible if only one gave it time, while she filled herself with so many interests, worries, concerns, and affections that she found it hard, to the point of intolerance and aggression, to give pride of place to one of the many people inside her. This often prompted confusion and vaguely directed emotional outbursts that were quite embarrassing. Embarrassing to me, primarily, though sometimes to her, as well.

One of her many sanctuaries was the kitchen. Although it was actually my kitchen, which I had set up according to my needs and which had grown with me through the years, she took over the space and its objects in no time. The knives had always been kept on the right-hand side of the silverware basket, because of the frequency with which I used them, but suddenly they were on the left, while the spoons, which she used more often, occupied the former knife compartment. Cups, plates, pots, and pans suffered the same fate. My favorite cup, an unmatching one that had its place beside the stove, was moved, as a punishment, because Judit wanted us to drink from matching cups, and as no pairs could be found in the cupboard, two identical new cups were purchased.

Every evening, Judit wrote in her diary for half an hour. It was a bulky little notebook. Because of the amount of ink they soaked up, the pages were wrinkled, so the book peeked open temptingly. There was no need for her to hide it, as it kept track in Hungarian of the story of Judit's suffering with a silent, stubborn, and contrary German composer. In fact, she often left it open on the kitchen table, to excite my natural curiosity. As my name was on almost every page, it was not hard to guess the source of her inspiration, and as my wickedness and my conscious self-effacement were often captured in direct quotations in German, its slant could not go unnoticed. It was a book about me, that much was clear. But why keep such careful track of what I thought about her and the rest of humanity? Why did posterity have to be told that I believed people could not live together? Judit was confessing, but to whom? Was she writing a diary in order to present it to Maria as proof of my artistic and human failure? It was strange, in the Hungarian text with its long, threatening words, to find my own threats, my fears, and my mockery—particles that, taken together, formed a picture of someone on the verge of destroying the world and himself. There was not one loving German word in those pages that might have suggested a normal person, only accusations, insults, dismissals. And in the middle of all that muddled scribbling I found, in German, a sentence attributed to me: If you do that, I'll kill you. It was repeated twice more on the same page, apparently as part of a commentary Judit had devoted to that outrage: If you do that, I'll kill you. When had I uttered that sentence? On a Sunday, the second Sunday we spent here together, as the date of the entry revealed. Did I really say that? I tried to remember the argument we'd had, about something musical it was, which I circumvented by saying: You are hopeless—words I found quoted on the next page of the diary. But why did I threaten to kill her? I left the house during the fight and went into town to have a drink. I came back later that night, and as far as I remember went to my study and fell asleep on the sofa; in any case, I woke up there the next morning. I don't know what you're planning to do to me, I was quoted as saying the next day, though I could not remember having said it (which, however, might be ascribed to my hangover). Was she planning to do something to me?

To hell with her and her daily confession.

24

In a few years, I will be referred to as a twentieth-century musician, and if I reach the twenty-first century, which seems likely, my obituary will say I was a typical representative of the music of the final years of the twentieth century, a composer who turned away from the new even when it was right in front of his face. His anxiety about abandoning the aural work of art made him lead a double life: on the one hand, he followed a moderate modernism, especially in his operas; on the other, he lived off of the countless compositions he produced for television, several of which became veritable hits. His most ambitious project was his Mandelstam opera, in which he attempted, with great effort and not without charm, to combine the century's centrifugal forces, both artistic and political, in one complex composition. Whether the abyss between the desire to represent the course of history as a political and social necessity and the realization of that desire in musical terms was successful throughout remains to be decided. However, the premiere in Nuremberg and the subsequent performances in Warsaw, Moscow, and Budapest were celebrated as the final high point of a dying opera culture. All in all, it should be remembered that he felt more strongly connected to the musical life of the east than of the west. In the last few years, not much was heard from him. The composer, who had lived in isolation in southern France since the turn of the century, rarely appeared in the music world, although his "Fragments" challenged interpreters again and again. His friends and associates were shocked to learn that he died by hanging himself in his house in France.

That's it. Or something like that. It can always be brought up to date, but that is the gist of it.

25

Since the previous summer, an old, half-ruined château near my house has been inhabited again. The new owner, a Paris lawyer, an aristocrat who has made his mark as a defense lawyer in the latest Nazi trials in France, is having it renovated. All the craftsmen and bureaucrats in the village are in a state of excitement because he is a man of means intent upon a faithful restoration of the huge structure. I have been following the progress with anxiety and mistrust because, given the size of the grounds, one has to assume that before long summer parties will be held there, quite possibly with dance music. The Count has three children of an age for parties; in fact, I have been observing them from afar with increasing loathing. Nothing is more appalling than having French aristocrats in the neighborhood, because such people attract their own kind. The French aristocracy might even be more appalling than the appalling German aristocracy, whose petty narrow-mindedness is unsurpassed in Europe. Plate collectors—they are all plate collectors, sitting on their wobbly but authentic little chairs, studying genealogical tables. So-called antiques lovers who have taken leave of their senses. Welcome party guests. If it gets really bad, they throw evenings of chamber music with an audience consisting exclusively of plate collectors bedecked with what's left of the family jewels. Some come all the way from South Africa, where they earn money as big-game hunters, just to attend evenings of chamber music. They love to tell stories about how unreliable black people are—they no longer say *Negro*. The French plate collectors have their problems with the North Africans, whose art they occasionally collect, but only the finest. When they are not busy with chamber music, the higher echelons of the European aristocracy are obsessed with African art. The thought that these people will soon disturb my solitude is unbearable, but there is apparently nothing to be done about it. I will have to let the hedge grow higher. And when the aristocratic lawyer's children have their parties, I will have to go to the police.

While I was still busy thinking about how I should deal with the new enemy, one of them invaded my garden. The son. Good-looking, as I conceded, much to my annoyance. Aquiline nose, pale eyes, gel in his hair, white shirt over shorts, barefoot. He was from next door, he said; could he use the phone? Jacques, the electrician, had accidentally cut their telephone wire. Feel free, I said, and pointed to the open front door, hardly able to speak, I was so angry. The phone's on the piano. I sat in my chair, trembling, unable to concentrate. Tomorrow, they will ask if they can use my water supply; the day after tomorrow they will want to borrow my garden tools; in two weeks, an offer to take over my house as servants' quarters for their North African slaves will land in my mailbox. You can leave the furniture in the house; the gardener will dispose of whatever the Tunisians have no need of. If you do not accept our fair offer, we will take legal steps, which, sir, can lead to . . .

I closed my eyes and sank so deeply into my enraged fantasies that Judit had to shake me. Philippe would like to thank you, she said; and when I opened my eyes, I saw Philippe's tanned hand in front of me, which I shook reluctantly. So Philippe is that dandy's name, I said to Judit after the young man had departed; let's hope he won't drop in every half-hour to snoop around our house.

You're revolting, Judit said. Unlike you, Philippe has good manners. We should invite him to dinner, so you can tell him something about the area.

Me?

Yes, you. He studies business at the Sorbonne and is interested in art and literature, and his two sisters play violin and piano. We can play music together.

Judit, I said, I don't want any businessmen in my house, nor do I want to play music with my neighbor's daughters. I just want to work in peace.

Work? asked Judit. Anyway, tomorrow afternoon, we're invited to the roofing ceremony, which all your friends from the village will be attending.

I was speechless. The pretext of wanting to use the phone had given the young man the chance to turn Judit against me. They had probably been meeting behind my back. Philippe! They may have even reached an agreement to drive me out of my house. They would probably occupy my property while I was at the party. The only hotelier in the village was arrested last year because right after his guests had filled out their registration forms, he would promptly pass them on to his accomplices, who would in turn rob the guests' homes while they stayed at the hotel. The trick was discovered because a couple from Aachen who had been robbed the year before spent the night in our village again and saw a painting that had been taken from their house on the wall of the provincial hotel's impoverished lobby, an early Baselitz that the new owners, unable to sell, had hung up in the bar—upside down. My piano will almost surely be suffering at the hands of the daughters before the year is out.

As far as I'm concerned, I growled, you can go to our enemies' party on your own.

But I said I'd be happy to come with my father, said Judit. What should I have said?

With her father! I spent the entire afternoon regaining my composure.

Judit actually did go to the party the following afternoon. My ears plugged, I sat in the garden and tried to work. The night before, I had hardly slept, my head buzzing with Judit's surprise comment. I found it harder to concentrate than ever. Listlessly, I read the history of Stalinist crimes, always the same terrible story, always ending with interrogation, torture, and death. The words had to be stripped of their bureaucratic screen. Name after name—one provincial governor after another turning over his list of candidates for death; it would be authorized; executions would follow with no court decision. The book said nothing about whether the party bigwigs, if they too were not executed, had to face charges in legitimate courts later, defended by people like my neighbor, because every mass murderer, no matter how brutal, has to be defended. If one could trust the account, everybody was dead in the end—except Stalin. I recalled my father saying at breakfast one day that Stalin had died. Nobody made a sound, no transports of joy. The family sat around the table, embarrassed, not saying a word. An evil, sick, tired statesman had died.

At some point, I could no longer stand the silence. I took the plugs out of my ears and stood close to the hedge, where I could watch the party without being seen. At the long tables in the garden, I could see the mailman, the mason with his wife, the electrician who had supposedly cut the telephone wire, the owner of the secondhand shop with his permanent smile (eager to dump his old, fake stoneware on the aristocracy, after I had refused to pay him twenty francs for the chipped plates), the vegetable lady, the cheese man, and a few others I only knew by sight. Judit was seated at the table with the nobility, Philippe next to her, bent over with laughter—she was probably telling him stories about her crazy stepfather. What else, in God's name, could she be saying that the aristocratic family found so amusing? There was nothing funny in her life, except for me. I had the urge to storm over and drag her away from that crew by the hair and back into my life.

I was still standing by the hedge, harassed by mosquitoes, when Chinese lanterns were lit and a small band began to play dance music, and Judit and her new swain began to spin on the lawn to the happy applause of the guests. It was no roofing ceremony any more, but a wedding, which became ever more evident when the second dance was led by Judit and the lawyer. The father-in-law seemed to like his beautiful Hungarian daughter-in-law, for he was clearly reluctant to let her fall back into the arms of the groom, who wandered restlessly around the dance floor until he could finally press his prize to his chest again, to his body. Was I only imagining it, or did Judit actually wave in my direction when a twist of her body made it possible, to give me a sign without irritating her new life partner?

About nine o'clock, I left my uncomfortable lookout with aching eyes, took my book, and went into the house, barricading the windows and doors. I did not expect anyone, nor did I want to let anyone in. I ate a few olives and some bread and salami, and drank a bottle of full-bodied red wine so I could fall asleep quickly.

At eleven o'clock the music fell silent.

At midnight, I heard a delicate laugh at the door, which grew louder and then ebbed again.

In the morning, having been startled awake by my inner clock, I found Judit asleep in her bed. I stood in front of her and stared, with all the tenderness and emotion I was capable of, and yet I would have liked to kill her.

Rigid, I went into the kitchen, where I found one side of a window open; then I made coffee and sat down at the table. Her diary lay there, wide open; in a long Hungarian sentence apparently scribbled down that night, I read the name Philippe de Gaillard.

26

Philippe came over almost every day. Sometimes he dropped by early in the morning and drank an espresso with us. Sometimes he came to lunch, and, of course, he joined us most evenings. Occasionally he brought me a book or an article about music that he had found in one of the many newspapers he apparently read. Judit had asked him to make suggestions regarding my French investments, which, she thought, were not working hard enough—yet another reason for him to visit. And from time to time, his bluestocking sisters followed him, to play chamber music with Judit and me. It was a beautiful, low-key summer.

Everyone seemed satisfied; only Judit worried me. By day, she was malleable, pliable, eager to please everyone—me, Philippe, the lawyer, her music; in the evening, when peace and quiet settled in, her face reflected a field of corpses, and at night, when, as had become my habit, I watched her as she slept, she looked as if she were resting on a pillow filled with dried peas.

Fall was in the air. The chestnuts were bursting open and spitting their brown fruit onto the ground, and the white mist that hung over the valley in the mornings broke up more sluggishly. The farmers harvested faded, listless sunflowers; the thick cornfields were thinned out; the red millet greedily gathered the last hot rays of the sun. A blue shimmer hung over the plowed fields, and clouds of gray smoke rose from the fires in the fields to the sky. Only the mulberry tree in front of the house retained the dark green lacquer on its leaves, as if it alone were unconcerned about the change of seasons.

We have to start thinking about leaving, I said to Judit, who sat at the kitchen table studying a score, as if her fire had gone out. Summer's almost over. Before her courses began, she wanted to go to Budapest: an uncle was turning eighty, which she could not miss under any circumstances. But you have to come, too, she suddenly said. I can't go without you. If you don't come, I won't speak to you any more.

What was I supposed to do in Budapest? Walk through the refurbished neighborhoods, look at the new McDonald's restaurants? The thought of celebrating Judit's uncle's birthday with her family was painful. And Maria? What would Maria say if I came back to Budapest as Judit's companion, twenty years late, an old Western European staying at the Gellert and paying with American Express?

I can't go to Budapest with you, I said lamely, I have to work. Maybe next year when the opera's finished.

Judit did not answer. Her shoulders began to twitch, then her whole body. As if with her last burst of strength, she leaped, pushed the chair aside, slapped her own face, and screamed and raged as though she were possessed by the devil. I said nothing. The outburst was too powerful for me to check it with a comforting word. So I remained a silent spectator of her suffering, which she apparently didn't want to share with me.

I have been afraid of such outbursts since early childhood. My mother, as well as several of my aunts, was subject to panic attacks; the family, mute attendants of those ghastly attacks, was never able to intervene. Afterward, once the situation was under control, the attacks were never mentioned, at least not around me. So I was not allowed to do anything, either, when my favorite aunt was committed to a locked ward where she lived for a few more years under observation, always friendly when I visited her, but absent. The dark foundation of her childhood has broken open, said my father. The war has come for its last victim, said my mother, who also suffered from depression and lay in bed with her eyes closed for weeks at a time.

At some point, Judit left the room. I stayed seated at the table, drank wine, and smoked. When Philippe appeared to take Judit for a walk, I couldn't say a word. I just waved in the direction of her room, assuming Judit had gone to bed, but he came back right away—he couldn't find her. We waited together in the kitchen for a while, then Philippe suggested we go look for her.

We parted ways in front of the house. Philippe walked toward the village; I took the path to the river. The moon was hidden behind clouds, so I moved slowly, stumbling. Bats and night birds were on the fly; an owl's hoarse hoot could be heard. The sloe bushes bordering the path rustled and creaked. It took me a long time to reach the river. No trace of Judit. I called her name, softly, but the only answer was the friendly sound of the river, happy to be carrying fresh water from the storms after the long dry summer.

An insurmountable distance separates me from Judit and her world, I suddenly thought. Even if I find her, I won't be able to reach her anymore.

I came at last to the little pedestrian bridge that took me to the other shore, where a narrow, slippery path led to the village. I was to meet Philippe there, in the Café des Sports in rue Gambetta, unless he had found Judit and taken her home. Judit, I whispered to the shadows that spread on the path as the clouds released the moon for a split second. Beyond a dark stand of trees was the village, which cast a pale light into the sky.

No Judit. I had already reached the plumber's and the tiny houses owned by the Arabs next door, which glimmered with the faint blue glow of television sets. A man was standing in his doorway, smoking; he gently raised the hand with the cigarette in greeting, and I raised mine without having recognized him. Through an open window, I saw the prime minister's head filling the screen; the sound seemed to have been muted, a measure I often take to protect myself from politics. On the lighted steps in front of the church sat a kissing couple, observed by an agitated dog. Without releasing his girlfriend's mouth, the boy suddenly raised a hand and threw a ball into the air, which bounced toward me across the pavement in small arcs. I stopped the ball with my foot, then kicked it against the wall of the church as hard as I could, where it re-bounded and vanished in a high arc into the darkness. The dog stood still, at a loss; I turned down rue Gambetta, at the end of which the Heineken's sign at the café was still lit. No Judit here either. The owner had not seen her for days. The two other guests, Pierre and Jean, two heavyset, bluff carpenters, indicated they had not seen her either. The two had worked in Africa on a construction site for the previous two years; now they could not fit into the nar-row world of the village and whiled away their evenings in the café, or went hunting. Pierre had won the local pinball championship, but not even his engraved silver cup could help him. They had Africa in their eyes and Africa on their tongues. Most of all they loved to talk about the African baobab, with which none of the local trees could bear comparison. I drank a Pernod with them, a glass of red wine, then a coffee. Still no Philippe, which I hoped meant he had found Judit.

After I had paid the tab, Jean took me home on his Vespa. As I squatted on the seat, Jean's rifle on my lap, I heard the café owner lowering his iron window bars with a crash, like prison gates closing behind me.

From far off, I could see the lights on in both Philippe's house and mine. A Schubert melody coursed through my head in an endless loop, but I could not remember the lyrics for the life of me. The two houses stood there in the blackness of midnight like two brightly blazing bonfires.

Jean dropped me off by my gate and sped off as if chased by ghosts before I had a chance to give him his rifle, a lovely weapon, which I carefully shouldered. Beside the

gate was a stranger's car, an old Peugeot, the motor cooling under the hood with quiet clicks. The cicadas were
going wild.

I walked into the kitchen. Philippe leaped up and ran
to me, his arms spread as if in apology, but stopped when
I slung the gun off my shoulder. The stranger, who had
been sitting in my chair, stood up too, and introduced himself: Bricault. He was the doctor from Auville; Philippe had
called him in because the old village doctor was undergo-
ing withdrawal treatment in the Vosges mountains, and no
one expected him to return. So now we had young, successful Dr. Bricault, a scrawny fellow careful with every
sentence, in love with his own originality, a perfumed,
pompous ass who, in response to my question about what
had happened to Judit, pushed me down into a chair and
calmed me, as if I were suffering from an incurable disease, as if the whole household were doomed and he was
the bearer of bad tidings. Philippe instinctively sensed that
my gorge was rising, and with a fearful look at my
weapon, pushed Dr. Bricault into another chair and dryly
related what had happened, repeating the parts I didn't understand in unison with the doctor. It was very simple.
Philippe had found Judit in a wood a hundred yards from
the house, a lost little bundle with no idea who she was,
sobbing on the ground and refusing to follow Philippe,
who had then gone to his house to call Dr. Bricault, who
gave Judit a shot of tranquilizer—A tranquilizer?—Yes, a
shot to calm her, you see, put in the doctor, demonstrating
the action of a hypodermic with his fingers. Then the two
of them had carried Judit to my house and put her to bed.

That was the comprehensible part.

But then the doctor stood up and proceeded to define the drama in medical terms, which automatically stripped it of some of its tragic and urgent quality. In any case, it was a nervous breakdown, a hysterical fit of the worst kind, which could not be treated with a mere shot. Bricault, happy to have a chance to be responsible for something other than boils and tonsillitis, recommended a clinic. Rest, rest, rest, under medical supervision; Judit must recover her vitality; she was at the end of her rope. Completely spent, drained, no reserves. If we did not do something immediately, Judit's life would be in danger.

I asked if I could see Judit. They agreed, but not before Bricault had once again described the patient's condition. If she opened her eyes, I was to leave the room at once. And say nothing; please, not a word.

We tiptoed into Judit's room, where a peculiar atmosphere prevailed, as if the young person who lay on the bed with her pointed features in a chalk-white face had just died. But she was alive, as I could see from the twitching hand sticking out from under the white sheet. To keep my balance, I carefully placed my fingertips on the tabletop. How long did the three of us men stand around the bed? A minute or an eternity? Philippe with his handsome, worried face, the possible lover and an easily imagined husband, if the board of directors of his aristocratic circle did not withhold its consent. Dr. Bricault, a man right out of Flaubert. And me? I had long since ceased to understand what my role in this provincial play was; in any case, I was the one most responsible. At the moment, I was the devil, the vampire who had sunk his teeth into the tender neck of innocence. After I had been allowed to play every possible role all summer long, I was now to end my career as the embodiment of evil. No applause at the end, no bows, no new part. I was just about to open my mouth, which seemed stuck shut, to whisper Judit's name, when the sick girl's eyelids fluttered, and I felt the tender pressure of Dr. Bricault's arm pushing me toward the door. I was no longer welcome. What's more, the two gentlemen decided to have the patient moved to the hospital, to neutral ground, as Bricault put it, where she could decide what she wanted to do and where she wanted to go. I no longer had a part in this script; I was eliminated. But of course I had to sign a release form: those were the rules of the game.

27

Some people can do anything, others next to nothing. All music history can be fitted into that pattern. Of the hundred musicians I have known well in my life, three made it. The others have been forgotten. A few became professors who still put a piece or two on paper in their free time, others landed radio jobs, still others married into money and could organize musical evenings at home for their relatives. I helped a Pole I considered the most gifted musician in our Warsaw circle to find a job as a répétiteur at the Munich Opera. His voluminous oeuvre is in boxes under the piano at his house. At the so-called summer courses in the south of France, I ran into a Hungarian who had caused a stir in the sixties with songs based on Endre Ady; he gave the tourists a chance to hear Beethoven's Opus 31, no. 2, outdoors, accompanied by airplane and cricket. He was my guest for two nights; then he had to go to his next concert, and four weeks later he took his own life. He was a musical genius who risked everything and lost everything. There is not a single note of his on the market, not one CD. I wrote a eulogy for him that nobody wanted to print, because everybody thought I had invented him. Only when I produced his essay on Karl Weigl was anyone inclined to see my friend as anything but a figment of my imagination, but since even Karl Weigl had been forgotten, there was good reason to erase the memory of Pál, too. When I sent my eulogy to the old address in Budapest, the letter was returned: Addressee unknown. This man whose music once had a place in the world has been lost for ever. Nothing is left of him but his death.

28

It was not unpleasant to be alone again. The bustle created by two or more people living together evaporates; the loud shouts and clatter, the eternal questions and admonitions die away. I worked, took care of the animals, went for walks. If left to one's own devices for amusement, one comes up with solutions that never materialize in a group. Some prefer company, indulge in marriage, or else take pleasure in sporting events or attend the theater. Some find it natural to dominate, others to help. Only a few people can be alone. And since they are so few, they are suspect. Following the events of the past few weeks, I felt I had become an object of suspicion. People I met in the café or while shopping or just passed while walking might say hello, but the way they did so made me think Dr. Bricault must have advised them not to come too close. Danger of infection. The less attention they paid me, the less I needed to explain; that was fine with me. Above all, I did not have to accept any expressions of sympathy. I had driven the woman mad; sympathy was inappropriate. It was clear who the victim was and who the culprit; that was how simple things were in this part of the world that I loved so much. What made my case more complex was that the victim was no longer visible. There was not a trace of blood, no weapon, no gravestone. Only my house, overgrown once again, and its inhabitant, who had finally shown his true face. And there were rumors, as Philippe told me with a certain pride.

Philippe and I had become friends of a sort. The one reliable thread connecting me to the world, he was a good, humorous storyteller. He told wonderful tales about his aristocratic aunts and how they clambered around in their family trees in the naive belief that they mattered. They were vain, good-for-nothing creatures of chance who had nothing but their names. The family had made common cause with the Germans during the war and had had to atone for it, and Philippe's father had defiantly become *the* lawyer who defended collaborators, although he was actually a weakling, a chicken, and a yes-man. Philippe's mother, however, whom I had seen once, from afar, was responsible for the artistic talent in the family. She had been trained as a pianist, but her chances had been ruined by gout. A little bit out of boredom, a little bit out of high spirits, and much to the horror of her husband, she had founded a private music school; in fact, the idea of buying and restoring a house in this godforsaken region actually resulted from Philippe's father's desire to keep his wife away from Paris.

Philippe had accompanied Judit from the local hospital to Munich in the ambulance. It is by no means easy to transport a Hungarian from France to Germany in an ambulance, but he took care of all the formalities. Philippe found a bed for her in a clinic; he gave the doctor Judit's case history; and, as someone who apparently talked to her on the telephone several times a week, he was also the one who convinced her to take a semester off and go back to Hungary for half a year. I may have been responsible for organizing Judit's life at the beginning, but Philippe had taken over the current, delicate phase. As the young man refused to let me reimburse him for his expenses, I only had to pay Judit's personal bills, which I was happy to do, especially since Philippe's advice had made my money do what, in Judit's opinion, it should have been doing all along: in other words, it multiplied, as the capitalist ethic requires. I would not have dreamed of prescribing such a course for my money, but Philippe thought otherwise. He always sent it wherever the action was, and it always came back with rich pickings. The director of the Banque Nationale Populaire was probably the only person in the village who had any respect for me—at any rate, he respected my bank account.

In mid October, Philippe was the last member of his family to leave for Paris. On the phone, he told me about the progress Judit was making. For me, the ban against getting in touch with her was still in effect; I was not even allowed to write her a letter. If Dr. Bricault had not occasionally come by for a game of chess, I would have spent days on end without hearing a human voice, which made the work on my opera extraordinarily productive. I could finally concentrate on my voices, which grew purer and clearer, and soon I was sure I would have something to show at the end of the year that would satisfy my own demands, and even Judit's. The complete solitude had made it possible for a quality to emerge that I'd no longer believed I had in me. The music that came out every day was original; its rules and blueprints existed in my head alone and grew from a singular experience. Whether my opera ever made it to a performance or not, I was proud that I had produced it. My confidence in the quality of my work was strengthened by the news that my composition "Quiet I–XV," a minimalist meditation in fifteen sequences for a changing set of instruments, was to receive an important prize in Chicago, which meant that interest in it among European ensembles would pick up. The ground for the opera had been prepared.

Bricault was a bad chess player, but a good loser. He tried to win, but he did not care whether the pawns fell, as long as the king survived. You're a provincial general, I told him once. You aim for higher rank, but you obviously don't value the lives of your troops. He was not insulted; on the contrary, he made another silly move that sacrificed one of his most valuable pieces. He wiggled his foot, played nervously with his hair, drummed his fingers on the tabletop—and made his next mistake. It's not unlikely, I suddenly thought, that his medical practice is organized along the same lines. But his sincerity reconciled me to him again and again—his admission that he was not a strategist, though he had always wanted to be one. The intimacy of our interactions increased alarmingly. One day he asked if he could bring a friend of his along, an Austrian he had met while mountain climbing. She loved Mozart, he said, but Alban Berg meant nothing to her; still, she was a gifted cook. In the middle of our meal at my house, Bricault was called to a patient, and all it would have taken was my consent for the woman to switch partners. She leaped up and embraced me from behind, because, as she put it, that had to be done once. When I did not move and left my hands lying on the table, she finally let go and sat down. I hope you won't think badly of me now, she said. I did not think badly of her at all, and told her as much. If Bricault doesn't come back, I said, I'll return your embrace. And then? she asked. Then he'll catch us. And then? Then I'll have to shoot him. And then? I'll hire you as a cook. And then, she said, you'll drive me mad, as you did Judit.

Fortunately Bricault came back soon afterward and took her with him. She left me her card—I found it under her plate when I cleaned up. A psychologist from Wels—I could have guessed as much.

By the end of October, the silence around me had assumed dangerous proportions. When the wind slammed a shutter against the house wall, I would be startled out of my wits, and when the cat that slept at my feet moved I would jump. It was time to be back among people. I copied my music in town and sent it to Munich; now it was time to close the house for the winter. As nobody in the village was willing to help with the garden, Bricault sent me a gardener from the next village, a friendly man I shared my lunch with. While he cut back the vines, I cleaned the house. I put it back the way it had been before Judit's arrival. I made it my house again. After five days, the gardener finished his work. I called Philippe in Paris to say goodbye and told Bricault I was going to Munich for the winter. I was barely able to keep him from coming over again. One last game, he pleaded, but I was firm. In May, I said; then we'll play again.

I packed the car so I could leave first thing in the morning. I delivered the house key and money to the woman who also took care of Philippe's parents' establishment, and instructed her to look after the animals. Then I got a blanket and lay down on the sofa for the night, as the bed was already stripped. I could not fall asleep.

A phase of my life was over. I had done everything I could to be unlike myself, but I didn't know whether I had succeeded. I was sure only that I no longer had things under control. As a child, I learned to keep things in perspective. As a teenager, I left nothing to chance. As a student, I was expected to pursue chance in order to put it to use in my work.

And now?

It was pleasant and liberating to have let chance in. It had knocked so lightly at the door of my life that I hadn't heard it. Now it had become almost a housekeeper in my life, or should I say a housemaid? A force, at least, that was playing with me, a force that would always be stronger than me. One day, I'll have to hide what I am from it, I thought. Then I must have fallen asleep.

29

The morning was peculiarly warm, too warm to leave. Perhaps the last warm front was arriving from the Pyrenees, a sigh before the rains. In any case, the bees were already working hard, and the salamander family that lived at the well had finished its breakfast. Be true, I bid them, as I heaved the cover over the well. The fog had made the valley a white wasteland; the blue and purple hilltops were free of it. A rude beauty appeared to the tired eyes that scanned the landscape with a feeling of gratitude. I brought the garden tools to the shed, which was still sticky and hot, as if it had slept through the change in the weather. Out of habit, I locked the shed, although any thief could have opened it with one kick against the rotten boards. Somehow, I had led an incomprehensible life here, although everything in it was actually simple and manageable. When I finally locked the last door, a fleeting pain ran through me. A part of me would stay behind in that house, although I had the sense I would never find room for it in my life again. We all leave part of ourselves behind when it no longer fits us, yet we feel poorer for its loss. Then there are those people who cannot part with anything. They never stop telling stories of their childhood, out of fear that they might lose it. They die clutching the very same teddy bear they grew up with.

Near Lyons, the traffic came to a standstill. Where in the world did all the trucks come from? Half the population of Central Europe appeared to be moving to southern France, Spain, or Portugal that October, while the southern Europeans were drawn north for reasons just as mysterious. An incomprehensible resettlement seemed to be taking place, a total trade-off, if in fact all the furniture trucks were carrying furniture. I would probably find Dr. Bricault in Munich. And of course, Bricault would insist on drinking French milk in Munich, if the milk trucks were actually carrying milk.

I reached Geneva in second gear, and all I saw through the stubborn rain was cars. By the time I reached Lake Constance it had cleared up; I was astonished to find that there was a reality beyond the highway, with houses, vineyards, and occasional cows, grumpy and contemplative in the last light.

I found a room in Bregenz. One of those sad rooms with brown carpets and birds on the wallpaper. And a television mounted on a swinging arm, so one can turn it on in the morning right after waking up. Seventeen channels, two of them playing my music. The little detective who had made me rich arrested a paralyzed wife for the murder of her husband's secretary. But the case had already been pretty much cleared up by the time I tuned in. The husband looked like a man who had no problem maintaining relationships with two women at the same time, a trait many people must find admirable, otherwise the topic would not have formed an episode. In front of him was the wife in a wheelchair, obviously longing for the shooting of the show to end so she could finally be on her feet again. She could not produce tears properly, so she hid her face in her hands and trembled. Just then a young woman appeared at my door with the sandwich and bottle of wine I had ordered from room service. To get some change from my jacket pocket, I literally had to hold on to her hip; otherwise, I would have pushed her onto the bed. Next time I'll get a double, I joked. My closing theme sounded, and I asked the waitress what she thought of it as I put the five-mark coin in her hand. She did not like any of it, said good evening, and disappeared. As she pulled the door closed behind her, I thought of Judit.

I made good progress on the highway to Munich. At Lake Ammer, I left the highway and took the country road through the bright morning. I listened to Wilhelm Kempff playing a Beethoven sonata on the radio. Departure and arrival became one, and tears almost came to my eyes. With some effort I got to my street, parked the car, and lugged the bags into the quiet apartment. I had asked Grützmacher to have the apartment cleaned, because I didn't know how Philippe and Judit had left it. Judit's cello was leaning against the dining room table, which had a large, colorful bouquet of flowers on it.

The mail was in my library on the little side table Judit had bought. I spotted Maria's letter immediately, fished it out, and put it aside. I crumpled the rest unread and threw them in the wastebasket. What else needed to be done? I picked up Maria's letter and read my name on the envelope, several times, as if I had to memorize it. I didn't have to open it—I knew its contents by heart, word for word. I sat there for a long time, quietly, and let the images run through my head. No reason to open the letter.

30

In the National Museum in Budapest, there is a strange drawing Maria and I looked at over and over again. It is in a display case in a dark corner on the ground floor, so one has to get quite close to make out the details. A female figure draped in a sort of toga made of soft, flowing fabric, her legs bent to the right. The woman looks sinister, with a raptor sitting on the wrist of her outstretched right arm and picking the flesh from her bones in an absentminded way. The threateningly raised index finger of the woman's left hand doesn't seem to bother him at all. To the right, behind the woman, is a boat. Did she arrive in the boat? Does she want to flee in the boat? At the woman's feet is a turtle, observing the scene with some interest.

That's me, said Maria, when we saw the drawing for the first time; my situation could not be defined more precisely than that.

As if spellbound, I stared at the little blue sketch, at the young woman's angry face, at her body.

Then I'm the turtle, I said, pleased with this division of roles. Maria was the angry woman; I was the peaceful, armored animal the raptor could not harm.

You're an idiot, Maria said; you're the raptor destroying me. I went to this windless island alone to find some peace and quiet, and was just undressing to lie in the sun. Look, my right breast is naked. I even turned the turtle away, so its ancient eyes couldn't see my heroic nakedness. And just as I was about to put my flowing gown on the ground so I could rest my head on it in the shadow of the boat, I heard a rushing sound in the air, which became a dry, spiteful clapping. That's the reason for the peculiar posture I have been given, even though I had just been kneeling. For as is plain to see, you seized my hand and dug your claws into my fingers, and then picked open the back of my hand like a vampire who's awakened an hour too late. Instead of relaxing, I'm now looking at your face with a gesture of horror, and my natural grace of a moment ago has swiftly turned into marmoreal cold. In this posture, I could just as well pass for a relief on a gravestone.

And you'll lie in the grave beneath me.